Budland

Tom Kranz

First Printing: 2017

ISBN 978-1-387-32525-2

Published by Tom Kranz Communications LLC
PO Box 42
Fanwood, NJ 07023

Prologue

I wish I could say that TV made me do it. That would be a cool hook to grab all those TV haters out there. And believe me, there are shitloads of haters. Hell, I can't stand to watch the news without yelling at the screen every single time myself. I evolved into a hater, which I am not proud of. I went to school to become an unbiased reporter, to write about things the way they really are, etcetera. Look at me now, for chrissake. But, I digress.

TV news didn't put me in jail. I did that all by myself. I survived, but things are different now. The question I still can't answer though: Am I different?

Borden "Bud" Remmick
Ardmore, PA

Chapter 1

Bud Remmick found it peculiar that one of the three people at the table in front of him chewed his gum so loudly and with such abandon that his action and sound filled the room. He wondered whether the gum chewer was a former smoker who, in another time, might have asked the other members of the panel for permission to smoke, or would he have just figured, fuck it, and lit up anyway?

The gum chewer was a man of about 40 with a Dick Tracy haircut and a shit-brown suit jacket that rode up his back, bunching up at the base of the neck. He wore a despicable, burgundy-paisley-over-beige tie, knotted in a careless double Windsor under an un-ironed, yellow shirt collar whose stays had long ago been lost.

He stopped chewing long enough to wrap his purplish lips around the opening of a plastic bottle of Poland Spring water, taking several drags that regurgitated back into the bottle each time he swallowed.

"Does the smoking bother you," Remmick imagined the guy would ask across the 15-foot open space between them.

"Um, no," Remmick would deadpan. "I like second-hand smoke and the way it makes my clothes smell."

The man took another swig as he gave Remmick a four-second, quizzical look, then took another and looked down at some papers, scratching his nose with a finger of the same hand that held the water bottle.

His two colleagues, a stocky, balding man with a body and hairline like George Costanza and a face like a relief map of the Moon, and a 40-ish woman with a severe face, white skin and red hair, shorn, Remmick figured, for delousing, sat squinting through the dust in the air. A sharp beam of sunlight cut a precise swath across the room diagonally from one corner up high to the opposite corner down low.

Remmick found himself feeling quite comfortable at that moment. The chair back actually was high enough. There was righteous thigh support. The arm rests were at exactly the right height and the solid, oaken seat was carefully machined to perfectly cradle an adult ass. The gray, mostly cotton jumpsuit was a definite improvement over the polyester, fluorescent orange number they first throw at the new arrivals, part of the initial hazing to establish early on that you are prison scum. And while Remmick found the cavity search and communal shower a hoot, he remembered how nothing locked him into his emotional cell more securely than the orange jump suit with the number sewn where the pocket should be and the letters NJDOC stenciled on the back. For the purposes of his little hearing, Remmick was instructed to wear the "dress gray", another convention designed, along with the lack of shackles and handcuffs, to make the whole thing seem more civilized—or at least, to make the bureaucrats running it feel more civilized.

The room was quiet except for the gentle sound of fingers leafing through papers in a folder-- my file no doubt, mused Remmick. George and the redhead sat with eyes staring off at a point somewhere way behind him, betraying no impatience, no annoyance, no nothing. Someone's cologne mingled with the musty smell of the ancient books that lined the walls and the damp odor of the yellowed ceiling that had obviously seen drier days.

The thumbing through papers stopped. The top was screwed onto the water bottle. Hands folded. Three sets of eyes clicked into place.

"Bordon Remmick," began the chairman in the cutting voice of an auctioneer.

Remmick nodded a bit and a remote control somewhere turned up the corners of his mouth slightly, bringing a faint light to his dim face.

"You've been here for one year," the chairman continued in a sing-songy voice with his hands folded. "Under the terms of your incarceration, you are eligible for parole."

He stopped and looked at Remmick with that quizzical, four-second look again, possibly his tiny brain resetting, then announced, "So far, your reviews are not good."

He looked down at the file.

"The officers report you are verbally abusive to them. You've been confined to your cell numerous times, denied meals, denied visits and phone calls."

Remmick wondered if all corrections officers were as thin-skinned as these overwrought pussies.

"You refuse to flush your toilet," he continued, "and the waste accrues until it reaches an intolerable level. Your cellmate is a reluctant participant in this ritual."

Remmick cocked his head ever so slightly. The waste accrues?

"You seem to enjoy masturbating without making any attempt to be, um, discreet."

There was that one time--

"The obscene phone call to the superintendent was particularly egregious," the examiner said, punching egregious as though delivering radio copy. Remmick turned alternate words over in his mind. He wouldn't have used egregious to describe that particular incident. Ingenious, perhaps.

The chairman reached down to scratch his ankle under his sock.

That day, Remmick called his wife collect from the pay phone as always. But this time, pushing the appropriate buttons on her office phone, Maggie conferenced him with the prison superintendent. Once she got past his secretary with her incredibly convincing sob story, the super came on the line.

The red-headed woman on the panel produced a portable cassette player, a cheap Radio Shack job, placed it on the table and hit the PLAY button. Remmick heard his own voice through the tinny speaker. She hadn't cued it to the beginning, idiot.

"--heinous rat fucker whose pimp boss in Trenton can't keep it up long enough to stay implanted in your rectum so can I please give it a try?"

At that point, a loud click was heard, then the end of any further sounds.

Red never broke her disapproving stare as she hit the STOP button.

Remmick's wife had laughed so hard, he thought she was going to pop a vein.

Egregious? Remmick thought not.

The chairman was not amused by his smirk.

"Do you think this is funny, Mr. Remmick?"

Remmick looked down at the floor for a moment to formulate. "Well, a little."

The redhead immediately broke her silence and practically jumped out of her skin.

"Mr. Remmick, you are here for killing a man, are you not?" she barked.

"I am," he answered without hesitation.

"Do you think that's funny?" she asked harshly.

Remmick stared for a moment at her thin, red lips, drawn onto that very white face under disapproving, squinty, hazel eyes.

"Funny?" Remmick repeated as his eyes wandered. "Well, not per se."

"Not per se?" she repeated incredulously, almost shrieking, the veins on her white neck popping.

"What the fuck does that mean?" blurted out George Costanza, shifting from one buttock to the other. "Is that supposed to be funny? Are you trying to be funny?"

Remmick really wasn't trying to be funny. But now, he was pleased.

"No sir," he replied with some sincerity. "What I meant was—"

He stopped short to assess the tenor of the room.

"What I meant was, I don't think it's funny that he died. But the way he died—well—"

He stopped, reconsidered.

"No," he resumed. "I don't think it's funny."

The chairman creaked back to life and leaned in to the exchange.

"So, you do feel remorse?"

"Oh, no sir," Remmick responded immediately and without emotion.

The three of them locked their eyes on him again and were quiet for another couple seconds until Red spoke up.

"And, you have no regrets about what happened?"

That took a moment.

"Yes, I do have a regret," Remmick said thoughtfully.

The panelists craned their heads forward in one motion to make sure they would hear it the first time.

"I regret that that pig fucker didn't know it was me who pushed that metal shelf full of Congressional Quarterlies onto his fat head."

Three looks of horror formed, as if digitally morphing.

"With one push and the power of gravity," Remmick continued evenly, "I erased that miserable cocksucker from the face of the planet. I don't think I'll ever be as pleased with any action as I was with that one. I don't know if it says so in that folder there, but later that evening, I went home and had one of the most sensational bowel movements of my entire life. Before flushing I took a farewell look, as I'm fond of doing, and was reminded of how easily it flushed away, just like that human turd got flushed away."

George Costanza broke his gaze and looked away. The red head remembered her mouth was open and closed it. The chairman never stopped looking Remmick in the eye.

"Alright," the chairman finally said. "I think we get the picture."

Remmick took a breath and said, "I hope there are no more questions about remorse and regrets."

The chairman shook his head slightly and cracked the vaguest of smiles.

"Mr. Remmick, I think we're done here. You'll have our decision before day's end."

"Goody," Remmick said with a smile.

A corrections officer appeared and beckoned Remmick to stand up. He applied the metal bracelets to his hands and feet, then connected it all with chains.

Remmick was amused by today's activity, but soon was back in his cell and the amusement wore off.

###

Chapter 2

It had only been a year since it all ended and he went away. Maggie wasn't crying that day. There was plenty of prep time and they had talked a lot about it. Going to prison was simply the next step in the journey for both of them. Morone's wife, on the other hand, was bawling her eyes out and Remmick was never quite sure whether it was because hubby was dead or because Remmick only got four to six with the plea bargain. Remmick didn't feel sorry for her. He figured anyone with the poor judgment to marry that prick deserved whatever happened to her. And maybe that was why Remmick felt haunted, because he didn't feel adequate compassion for the Widow Morone. And children? There had been a mention of a grown child, a son, during the sentencing but he never surfaced.

Remmick was surprised at how quickly he got used to his cell and swell roommate, Levon Samuels. Levon was a black man who converted to Judaism to keep his wife happy several years before running her down with his Suburban in a Wendy's parking lot.

"I just meant to scare her," he was fond of saying. "I kind of misjudged that big fucker's brakes."

The size and weight of the Suburban notwithstanding, the jury seemed to think Levon ran her down on purpose and convicted him of voluntary manslaughter. He got 15 to 20.

Remmick considered himself lucky. He was 45 and with good behavior and time served, he could be out in a few years and still have his life. What would he be doing during that time anyway, he thought—working for that prick Morone? Driving two hours a day over the worst highways in America to go to a job he hated? He rationalized that it was far more desirable to share a little cell with Levon Samuels and eat meals off stainless steel trays than to continue to carry out Ronald Morone's orders. The only orders Ron Boy was giving now were to the fire demons who delivered diet Cokes and tuna wraps to his flop-house in Hell.

Of course, Remmick had plenty of time to think about things—mostly, was it worth it? Was it worth the pause this would put into his life to erase one destructive maggot from the planet? At the time, the answer was yes. But the first year went by slowly, and the parole board, as Remmick found out later that day, was not impressed.

Back in the pre-prison days, Bud Remmick had what any civilian would have considered a successful career in broadcasting. He was a senior producer at Kaleidoscope News following a couple harrowing decades in local television in Philadelphia. There, he learned to steal news only from good newspapers, like the Inquirer and the Wall Street Journal. He was an assignment editor most of the time, figuring out which stories to cover mainly by figuring out which people quoted in newspaper articles would be the easiest to find. Once his station interviewed them, it could call the story its own without having to do any annoying research or original reporting. He often wondered if the writers at the Inquirer ever got pissed when they saw their stories, right down to the grieving moms and self-righteous community activists, show up that same night on the 5 o'clock news. But Remmick didn't wonder long because he didn't really care.

Remmick's resume, with 12 or so years of assigning and producing in the nation's fifth largest television market, caught the attention of Steve Kronenberg, news director at Kaleidoscope, a fledgling network taking on CNN in the 24-hour cable news business. He and Remmick hit it off immediately during the interview, but he had to bring him up for two more interviews because Remmick didn't say much. Kronenberg later told Remmick he wasn't good at selling himself and he wasn't sure whether he was just going through the motions or really wanted the job. During the third interview, he was convinced Remmick really wanted the job because he bagged the tie and jacket and showed up in jeans and a three button pullover shirt.

Remmick was Kronenberg's coordinating producer on the overnight shift. There was a small news set with small lights and a small control room designed for three people to do a newscast on a shoestring. The most expensive thing on the set was the giant K logo, an attempt at elegance that reeked of self-loathing, but with an artistic flair.

The line producers and writers were women except for Remmick. The control room crew was all male, so it became Remmick's refuge for discussing hockey, women and sexual deviance. Remmick often mused that if he could have smoked, gambled and masturbated in there, he would have. He'd never had any problem working with or for women. He very much enjoyed every conversation he'd ever had about hormones, menstruation, the glass ceiling and asshole boyfriends. He even started getting a feel for the whole shoe thing. But from time to time, he had to escape to a man place.

Kronenberg gave Remmick the latitude to chase stories he thought were relevant to the overnight audience. In addition to the requisite interviews with Middle East scholars on the Palestinian question and the resident expert on terrorism, Remmick made it his business to find the cop who acted as the spokesman for the steering wheel thing called The Club. Yes, he explained, The Club is only a deterrent, as there is no foolproof device to prevent auto theft from a lowlife hell bent on stealing your car. You couldn't get this kind of information just anywhere.

Remmick also thought the world needed to know about Beano and why someone would invent it and whether it worked at all for larger people. So, he invited the head of the company to come in one night for an on-set interview. Sensing a theme that needed in-depth exploration, he also invited a woman who invented a yuppie fertilizer called Zoo Doo, a product that came in a delightful little plastic container with a cartoon of a caged elephant on the label. At a suggested retail of $5.99 a pint, along with Beano at $7.99 for four ounces, it was a celebration of all that makes life in America worth living: bowel movements and capitalism.

The segment made Kronenberg positively giddy and became the standard by which all overnight feature segments would be judged.

Unfortunately, Remmick was never able to equal that masterstroke because one day he arrived at work to the news that Kronenberg had been fired. There was no good bye, no warning, just a two sentence email addressed to all.

It said the new boss was Ronald Morone, a manager who had come to Kaleidoscope's humble newsroom from the recently defunct TeleFaith network, a 24-hour Christian channel that went belly-up despite Morone's heroic efforts to cut staff, cut expenses, cut original programming and increase revenue stream by packing the air with infomercials. A Google search of his name revealed an article in the New York Times about TeleFaith, written some months ago, in which the writer spoke to employees who anonymously reflected on their boss. Words that kept popping up included arrogant, brusque, bully and cold. One fired worker called him Satan. Another referred to an incident during which Morone called her into his office, closed the door, spoke to her in a voice that slowly escalated in volume and intensity until, about 60 seconds into it, his face was so red and his neck so distended, she thought he would explode from the neck up.

"Imagine Fred Flintstone with a tie and jacket screaming 'Wilma!' six inches from your face for 20 minutes," the anonymous woman was quoted.

Morone was quoted, too.

"I have a business to run," he said. "This is a business and the people who work here are the moving parts. It's that simple. If people can't deal with that, I'm sorry. As for my management style, this is the way I'm wired."

Three months after that article appeared, TeleFaith went off the air. A few months later and Morone was now Remmick's boss.

Thus, my-way-or-the-highway was born at Kaleidoscope News.

During one of his regular visits to Morone's office, Remmick spied a stack of Congressional Quarterlies on a small table behind his desk.

"Do you collect those?" Remmick asked.

Morone looked up blankly and said curtly, "I read them."

Remmick was not proud of the fact that he disliked Morone from the moment he read about him on the Internet. It would have been much fairer, Remmick reasoned, if he had given him a chance to be an asshole in person first.

In the confines of Morone's small office there was an indefinable smell. Morone was clean and moist, a bundt cake packed into a dull gray suit, starched white shirt and muted burgundy tie. His fleshy head wore the haircut of a 6-year-old boy, circa 1957. His fingers-- skin casings loaded with meat-- pawed through a periodical. There was no clutter, just a spare desk with a calendar, a laptop computer and six small TV monitors on a credenza against the wall. Remmick's quick glance noticed CNN and Kaleidoscope on two screens. The others had various other video sources, including Dr. Phil.

"You wanted to see me?" he asked without looking up from his CQ.

"Yea," Remmick said, standing at the door. "I think Bonita should go to Jerusalem for the Ariel Sharon death watch. Even if he doesn't die, there'll be interest for a few days at least."

The Israeli Prime Minister had just had a life-threatening stroke.

"Fine", Morone replied without expression. "Cost?"

"We'll split the satellite truck on the ground with the Tel Aviv bureau. Transmission to the States is basically free through London, up-linked to our transponder on L-Sat. Of course, the business class tickets will be pricey. JFK to Tel Aviv round trip will be about nine-grand.

"Business class?"

"Company policy says if it's seven hours or more, they can fly business."

"Each?"

"Bonita and her photographer."

"Of course."

"And the hotel room-- only the King David is available at the moment, 350 US a night. It's a ball breaker, but what else can we do?"

"Nothing," he agreed. "Do it."

Morone was good at these all-business conversations.

"Oh, and..." Remmick let it hang for a second.

Morone looked up after a moment. It was the first time their eyes met.

"Um, Bonita is hoping to be back by Sunday. Her boyfriend's birthday is the next day."

"No promises. She's a reporter. Let her report. I could give a shit about her boyfriend's birthday."

Remmick had no response. Morone seemed like he wanted to say one more thing. He did.

"Boyfriend, huh?"

With an absent grin, he picked up a remote and pointed it at one of the monitors.

"I could fuck her into next week," he offered while changing a channel.

Remmick stared at him. Morone didn't look back at him, only at the TV's as he clicked the remote. After another moment, he put the remote down and returned to his CQ.

"Then, we're off to Tel Aviv," Remmick offered as a closer and turned deliberately to leave the office.

Morone's head was again locked between hands as he seemed to read his Congressional Quarterly with gusto.

###

Chapter 3

As medium security prisons go, King's Point seemed OK, Remmick had concluded. He had nothing to compare it to, of course, but he got fed, got out of the cell each day, could read and watch TV and made collect calls on a pay phone. CO2 even allowed him to have a laptop computer for a couple hours a day. The officer would check each evening to see what he was writing about. He also told him if they ever found parts missing or the housing damaged, there would be no more laptop. He was evidently concerned Remmick might make a weapon out of a piece of plastic. It never even occurred to him

There were about 700 inmates in the facility, a brand new prison built four years earlier. Overcrowding was not yet an issue. There were plenty of corrections officers and they didn't seem to whine much. In fact daily conversations between CO's and inmates sounded very much like conversations between neighbors or business acquaintances. The CO's did their jobs and the inmates did theirs, moving around on cue, eating when told, etcetera. They followed the rules. With the addition of a healthy little dose of fear, order was achieved.

So, it was with some consternation that the prison superintendent greeted Remmick's first-year antics. Of course, Remmick wasn't under any illusions about why he was in jail. He knew he'd killed a man, though as he had told himself many times it wasn't his intention to kill him. Still, Remmick had trouble feeling remorse, as the parole board found out, and he had trouble kissing ass—anyone's. It was a lifelong struggle for Remmick, knowing the right moment to pander. He rarely found a right moment and tended instead to veer to the opposite extreme. Making statements seemed important to him, especially now that he had nothing else to do.

"How'd it go with the board today?" asked Levon a moment before taking a death drag on a Kool.

"I think I made quite an impression," Remmick answered dryly without looking up from the crossword puzzle on his laptop screen.

"Did you say you were sorry?" Levon asked with a grin.

"Not in so many words," Remmick answered through a faint smile. "They were a little unhappy with me".

Levon chuckled at that one. "That would be an understatement," he offered, then took another hard drag on his cigarette. "You even pissed off CO_2 when you jacked off all over the place."

CO_2 was the nickname for corporal Manny Trujillo, second in charge of the guards on the tier, a fairly easy going man who never got mad at anyone.

"Yes," Remmick agreed. "Maybe I'll stop that."

"I don't really give a shit," said Levon quickly.

"I appreciate that, Levon. Thanks."

Levon had made it crystal clear from their first day together that he had no interest in any kind of sexual exploits with Remmick or any other male. The same went for Remmick. So, at times of severe need, they agreed that one does what one has to do and that would be the end of it. In hindsight, Remmick admitted, it might not have been the best choice to stand there at the cell door as CO_2 walked by, timing the ejaculation to the exact moment of his passing.

"I actually wrote a little note to him on the laptop," Remmick said while typing. "I'm sure he'll find it tonight."

"Is it clean?"

"It says I'm sorry."

"Well, then…"

There were quite a few times when Remmick found himself giving Ronald Morone the benefit of the doubt. His day to day business decisions seemed sound. He left most of the human resources decisions to, well, humans. He counted on his senior managers to deal with all the messy stuff like vacation requests, pleas for comp time and the periodic emotional breakdowns that highly stressed news people tended to have. Days often passed without a Morone sighting. Things seemed to work fine those days.

Other days, the darkness hung in tapestries.

One such day, Hilde Schimmel sat at her newsroom work station, valiantly trying to log a Bush speech through tears that welled up, fell to her cheek, then welled up and fell to her cheek in an endless cycle. Her fingers typed Americans are steadfast in their resolve as she sniffled through her runny nose. Her right hand left the keyboard fast enough to wipe away tears, then returned in time to type we have more work to do there. She hit the ENTER key, which recorded the time of the sound bite, then resumed typing as Bush said we will not forsake the Iraqi people. She paused as the audience applauded, then typed applause, ENTER.

Her hands fell to her lap and she stared at the computer screen and the image of the president nodding. New tears fell, propelled by energy that she had kept locked away for months. She sat alone.

Remmick watched her the whole time. It would have been convenient for him to say he had just happened to glance in her direction but that would have been a lie. He thought Hilde Schimmel was the only certifiably hot woman in the whole newsroom, from her blond head down to her backless heels, inclusive of perfect teeth curtained by natural, indifferent lips.

He was standing in the doorway of his office which opened onto the newsroom, staring at her. The six or seven other producers were busy being busy. Hilde was oblivious to all.

Remmick turned back into his office for a moment, found a leaf of blank paper in a drawer, tore off a corner and balled it up tightly. He returned to his spot at the open office door, making careful calculations for the proper arc to land the missile in exactly the correct spot. There was a risk that the whole operation would be misinterpreted as a hostile act, but he had to take that chance.

Hilde sat weeping quietly with her hands in her lap, surrounded by empty space. She suddenly felt a light tap on the top of her head and saw the pea-sized paper ball airborne as it bounced off her blond dome and onto her keyboard. At once her head twitched slightly, the pallor on her face broke and her lips parted to reveal perfect, gleaming white teeth and a small space between the uppers and lowers. It was the faintest of smiles. She didn't look around. She didn't have to. Instead she inhaled deeply and let out a sigh heard, specifically, by Bud Remmick.

His eyes were locked on her, examining her reaction, hoping it was not one of disgust, disdain or despair.

She finally cocked her head a bit and turned her eyes so they looked at him through slits. To his infinite relief, there was a smile on her face.

Remmick looked at her innocently, shrugging. "What?"

Her lips moved

"Did you lose this?" She held up the paper projectile.

"Oh, yes," Remmick responded.

She dropped it into the trash can that was near her feet. She inhaled a medium inhale and drew her hands from her cheeks up over her eyes across the sides of her head and ears and back down until her face rested perfectly on a V formed by her hands. She stared straight ahead again.

"I don't know what to do," she said in a small voice.

Remmick walked over towards her, close enough to have a muted conversation, but no closer.

"There's only one thing to do," he responded. "Or it'll never end."

She looked up at him, full on, her eyes meeting his.

"That's easy for you to say."

"Of course, it is," Remmick said without argument. "But that doesn't make it any less true."

She continued looking at him but her gaze softened. It always did. A rerun of a conversation they'd had several times before.

"I have no problem working hard," she said. "I have no problem earning my way."

"I know."

She looked into his eyes for an answer.

"Then why must he own me?"

Remmick knelt down so his eyes were about level with hers and only she could hear him. Their eyes never unlocked.

"Because he is an evil fuck," he said in a low voice, lips barely moving.

It hung there for a moment. He continued.

"He doesn't give a shit whether you work for it. It's not about your ambition or your ability or your talent. He wouldn't know talent if it bit him in the ass. It's about his control over you. He wants you to know who's boss."

She blinked once and looked away.

"I know all that," she conceded. "He's in control, god damn it. What more does he want from me?"

"Evidently, he wants whatever you won't withhold."

She didn't respond. Remmick went on.

"What would be the worst thing that would happen if you told the truth?"

"That I didn't really graduate college? That I lied on my application? That Ronald Morone has been blackmailing me for five months?"

"Yes. What would be the worst that could happen?"

There was a resigned smirk as she looked down.

"I'd get fired, for sure."

Remmick couldn't argue that.

"It would be my word against his on the sex."

Remmick thought about that one.

"I'd be branded a lying slut and never work again in broadcasting."

She began to well up again with those words.

"Well, hold on," he jumped in quickly. "Never working again in broadcasting would not necessarily be a bad thing."

He was trying to be wry. She was having none of it.

"As for a lying slut," he quickly added with a grin, "well, I would never call you a slut."

This elicited a sheepish grin from a place they had been before.

"But a liar, maybe?" she asked.

"Well, you did say you graduated cum laude from Penn, for Christ sake. I mean god damn, did it ever occur to you that someone might actually check that out?"

"No," she conceded. "It really didn't."

"So," Remmick answered while standing up. "Lessons learned and life goes on. It seems, however, that the punishment does not fit the crime. It's one thing to lose your job over lying on an application. It's another to be sexually extorted."

Hilde had evidently had enough of this conversation for the time being, having had it several times before. She dabbed her eyes and pulled out a compact, touching up and inspecting her face from hairline to neckline. She then snapped the container shut and stuffed it in her bag.

"Hey," Remmick injected as she stood and prepared to turn away.

She looked him in the eye, searching for, something.

It was there, like always.

"Thank you," she said under her breath as she turned and walked away.

Visiting day was always a tedious mixture of excitement and melancholy. There was a coldly lit common room. CO's were everywhere. Every visitor was patted down twice and all parcels and bags were locked up in another room. There was a lot of anticipation, excruciating waiting and an inevitable emptiness.

Maggie came every Wednesday. She was always seated at a metal table with a smile for her husband. She was tough and tender, blonde and not as pretty as a year ago. Remmick knew this all hurt her much more than she let on. They always hugged hard and looked into each other's eyes for a good, long minute, making sure everything inside was still intact. He never saw the light go out.

They hadn't yet sat down after today's hug when she blurted out, "Did you really jerk off in front of a guard?"

Not the first words Remmick expected, but so be it.

"Oh hi, Honey Bunny," he chortled cheerily. "I'm fine, thanks."

She gave him a scolding look.

"Did you?"

He tried to look pouty and hurt and kicked a couple of imaginary rocks.

"Yes," he said quietly.

"Why did you do that?" she asked incredulously.

"I dunno," he responded. "Felt like it. I was pissed and bored and all worked up over memories of you."

He peeked up at her, looking for a sign. Instead, she sat down hard.

"Oh, my," he said. "Took your breath away, eh?"

She sat with her arms folded and looked away. Remmick sat across the table from her and spied a CO staring at them.

She looked her husband in the eye.

"Is this the way it's going to be for the next three years," she wondered.

"What way?"

"This, this shit with the jerking off and the overflowing toilet and the belligerence and the god damn—"

She stopped before finishing. Actually, she was finished.

He reached across the table for her hand. She reluctantly let him take it.

"No," he said. "It's not going to be this way for three years. I do get it, really."

"Sometimes, Bud," she began. "I don't know. You treat this like it's another affront against you, like these people put you here."

This was an unfamiliar tone.

"I know why I'm here," he reminded her. "I think about it every day, like I have a choice."

Her face softened a bit.

"But I can't help it if I'm not staying awake at night mourning that fucker's death. What I told them in the hearing room was absolutely true: I don't feel any remorse. What do you want me to do? It wasn't my plan to kill him, but that's what happened. Sucks for him and that's why I'm here. I get it. It's just not breaking my heart, Mags."

This was not what Maggie wanted to hear, evidently. She inhaled deeply and looked beyond her husband at a point on an imaginary horizon.

"This first year," she began, "it's been harder than I ever imagined it would be."

She started searching her pockets for a cigarette.

"No smoking here, sweetie," he reminded her.

"Yes, fuck, I know."

Her hands had pulled away.

"None of our friends talk to me," she resumed. "None of them, not even Mark and Christine. I'm not sure whether they're afraid to ask how I'm doing or if they really don't want to know. The neighbors go out of their way NOT to look at me. Jen at The Clipper doesn't talk while she's doing my hair any more. Jen not talking-- what the fuck."

If she had found a cigarette, it would be smoked half way down by now.

"I give us another two months, maybe, before the money runs out-- the house, my car, the god damn Verizon FIOS bill. I don't see getting a raise any time soon. Nineteen bucks an hour only goes so far, you know?"

Desperation was welling up in her voice.

"I'm scared," she said without emotion. "I'm scared we're going to lose everything."

She didn't dare to cry. She looked way past him.

"I never thought it would be like this," she said as her eyes relocked onto his.

All those talks they'd had about not caring what the rest of the world thought drifted away. It was obvious Maggie cared very much what the world thought. And why shouldn't she? The collateral damage of her husband's incarceration was beginning to collect on her shoulders.

"We can get new friends," Remmick began. "You can get a new hairdresser. You can sell the house and move somewhere else. None of that shit matters, as I thought we agreed months ago."

"I never thought it would be this hard," she said from a distance. She seemed like she was making up her mind about things. "Bud, the rest of the world doesn't view what happened as a just end for a nasty guy. It thinks you did a crime and you belong in jail. The long discussions about intent and being pure of heart and starting an adventure behind bars mean nothing to them. That's your little novel. It's not reality."

She reached into a back pocket and pulled out a folded piece of paper.

"This is fucking reality," she said, holding it up for him to see. The CO 30 feet away peeked over at them. Remmick took the paper and unfolded it. Inside, the word "KILLER" was neatly written with a black Sharpie.

"It was on my windshield when I went to my car after work last week," she moaned. "It had to be someone who knows me, probably passes me in the fucking hallway every day."

Her voice rose a bit and a CO came over to visit.

"You have to keep the volume down," he said simply.

Maggie collected herself quickly.

"Sorry," she said as her eyes sank to the floor again.

Remmick felt something he hadn't felt in months—uncertainty.

"What do you want to do, Maggie?" he asked cautiously. He was afraid of the answer.

` She breathed-in heavily, then exhaled loudly as she looked off into space.

"I don't know, Bud," she answered. "I need to think about things all over again. This is not what I expected. At all."

She gathered herself and leaned over to kiss him. He grabbed her and held her head, hoping the kiss wouldn't end quickly. But it did. She pulled away, stood up and walked towards the door.

Bud Remmick sat at the bare, metal table, alone.

He entered prison at 270 pounds. After a year, he dropped 50. The food wasn't awful but there wasn't a lot of it. That was alright with Remmick, though, since he figured there was no better time than now to lose weight. Even at over six feet tall, he couldn't pull off 270 pounds without looking, well, fat.

Exercise was one of the allowed activities and he did it almost every day, mostly fast walking and weights, just like he used to do at the Y. Some of the guys in the gym were buff beyond reality. What exactly were they getting ready for, he wondered?

There were no fat guys in prison, at least none who had been there for any length of time. Exercise was a mantra. It burned minutes one might otherwise use thinking about home. It diffused anger and negative energy. It was something to do.

One guy, Ralph Vignola, had a body that bulged so much with muscles, Remmick imagined he must be in pain. He was only about 5'6" but had a body built for heavy use, a thick neck that fused with his head and a small, almost dainty waist. Ralphie Vig was a former broadcast engineer with NBC on an extended stay at King's Point following an argument in the bowels of 30 Rock that ended with a broken neck for the other guy.

"I didn't mean to break his neck," he told Remmick once while spotting him on the bench press. "He kept brushing by me, pushing me back farther each time, to see how much I would take. He was a body builder too, see, and he thought because he was bigger, he could mess with me. But he didn't know I had a temper."

Ralphie stopped at that point, never fully explaining how he had broken the man's neck, only that the man lived. Remmick didn't really need the details. All he knew was, Ralphie was nice to him. Having worked in broadcasting gave them something in common, so Ralphie gave him weight training tips, spotted him on some of the equipment and generally offered a sympathetic ear. While it was obvious he was a powerful man, Remmick never would have guessed he was capable of breaking someone's neck with his bare hands. This piece of information was always top of mind whenever he interacted with him. The fact was, Ralphie was nice to everyone. He had no reason to be otherwise. He was the undisputed king of the gym. Everyone gave him his space. He seemed to belong to no specific group. He was just there, doing his 8 to 10.

"I'll tell you what," he said one day, "I got no worries. No worries at all."

"Why is that?" Remmick asked.

"This is me cleaning the slate," he explained. "Everything bad happened already. All the losses are, um, lost."

He picked up a couple of small dumb bells and did some bicep curls while talking. "It's all out there, you know? Everything I did and why. It's done. Now, I'm starting over."

"And you'll be a better man for it?" Remmick queried.

He never stopped curling. "Hey, I'm already a good man-- seven, eight, nine, ten." He put the weights down on the floor, breathing hard while looking up at

Remmick. "I just got a temper. You know, like that guy Posey in The Dirty Dozen."

"Except in your case, the guy lived."

"Correct," he said with an index finger pointing at Remmick's chest. "And that was a gift."

Remmick nodded slightly in agreement and said, "Amen, brother."

"Don't mock," Ralphie said with mock consternation. "Another quarter inch and his neck would have broken in the wrong place and he'd be dead or paralyzed. It was a fuckin' miracle, I'm tellin' ya."

Then he added, in a lower voice, "I couldn't do hard time, man. Life in a place worse than this? I'd have to kill myself."

Remmick had no doubt he was totally serious.

"And then I would be deprived of your company," Remmick said optimistically.

This elicited a grin. "Yes, you would," Ralphie Vig said. "Now why don't you go fuck off and bother someone else for a while?"

Remmick found his way to the wall-mounted weight device and he began to slowly pull the cable that lifted weights off the floor, flexing his arms and breathing deliberately in the process, unaware that Ralphie was eyeing him.

"Why are you here," Ralphie suddenly asked.

"Manslaughter," Remmick answered.

"No," he said. "I mean why are you here?"

Remmick stopped for a second and stared at him.

"Manslaughter," he repeated.

Ralphie wasn't looking at him. He was tending to a sore knee, rubbing it with his hands while flexing it as he sat on the bench. He grimaced a little, and then inhaled loudly.

Remmick resumed pulling the weights, holding them for 10 seconds at a time as he had been instructed, then slowly releasing them. This went on for some time.

Ralphie stood, still flexing his knee, then turned and watched Remmick for a few seconds. Remmick caught him looking and said, "What?"

Vignola stared at him for another second or two, then said, "You need to know why you're here."

Remmick gave him a studied and well-practiced incredulous look.

"I told you, man, I--"

"Yea, I know," he interrupted with an impatient nod. "Manslaughter."

Remmick decided this time, he would not respond but kept pulling the weights.

Ralphie picked up his towel with his right hand and tossed it over his left shoulder and slowly walked toward the shower area. He didn't look back.

Remmick watched him walk away.

###

Chapter 4

There was no greater waste of emotional energy, than the daily morning meeting at Kaleidoscope News. Morone insisted on gathering every living soul he could find and forcing them all to sit in a horseshoe around the small desk in the conference room at which he would station himself. He would already be there, tapping away on a Toshiba laptop, while the rest wandered in, bleary-eyed and toting coffee cups filled with tepid gray liquid. Senior producers, special events producers, line producers, associate producers, assistant producers and the chief technician, about a dozen people in all, made the daily pilgrimage. The room always smelled faintly like something electrical was burning. The fluorescent ceiling lights were bluish bright. It was always silent except for the sound of Morone's tapping away on the keyboard. He never looked up from his screen as the chairs filled up.

Remmick tried to be the last one into the room to save himself the discomfort of having to breathe the same room air as Morone for a second longer than necessary. Remmick's entry was usually the cue to begin.

He usually said something like, "Morning, all", as he shuffled papers. There may, or may not have been any responses. There was never one from Morone.

Remmick would go down the list of the day's top stories and how they might be covered, who might cover them, why they should be covered at all. Occasionally, a discussion would break out over a point of controversy.

"Hang on," Morone would say, holding up a hand but never looking up from his screen.

Silence would fill the room.

"What are the moving parts?" would be the inevitable query. His use of the word "what", rather than "who", was no accident, Remmick concluded. He would then run down which reporters and photographers were available.

"Morgan and Stein do Texas flooding," Remmick suggested. "They're only about an hour away by car. Shelly and Richie can return to the cop trial today. It's just downtown here and they can get on TV for noon."

Morone sat with his head cocked, evidently listening.

"Bonita and Stephen remain in Tel Aviv for the Sharon death watch. I think he'll live forever. They could leave today."

Morone looked up at Remmick. "Let's keep them through Sunday," he said, watching for Remmick's reaction. "They can travel home Monday, be back in the office Tuesday."

"We could comp them Tuesday, give them a day to turn their body clocks around," Remmick offered.

"I'm not paying them to sit at home," he responded flatly, looking back at his computer screen.

Remmick pressed on.

"Melinda and Max are on a plane now to Seattle for that school metal detector story."

Morone paused to ask, "What's that?"

"Mid-Valley High, where the school shootings were three months ago? They're installing metal detectors today and the school community is split about 50-50 on whether that's a good idea."

Morone chuckled lightly and said softly, "Fucking morons."

Several in the room strained to hear him. A few looked at each other.

"Levin, Powelton and Jameson are off today. That's everyone," Remmick said with finality.

"Fine," Morone said. "Here, I want you all to see this."

He motioned to the 27-inch television that sat on a wheeled stand next to his desk. He turned it on. As the picture appeared, it revealed a still frame of a woman. He aimed the remote and pushed PLAY.

"We're interviewing her today," Morone said flatly.

The tape played, revealing a face familiar to all in the room, a regular reporter on CNN. Morone sat motionless, watching TV. After about two minutes, he stopped it.

"She's good. Nice mouth," he offered. "With bigger tits and a haircut, she'd be better."

He solicited no opinions and none were offered.

Morone folded down the screen of his computer, gathered a couple of items from his desk and got up.

"Carry on," he said absently and walked out of the room.

The rest sat silently, some still gazing at the dark TV screen, some looking at each other. No one said a word.

By lunchtime Remmick had noticed that Hilde hadn't shown up for work. This was unusual. In her seat was a part timer named Gwen, a nice enough young woman, who was logging the daily State

Department briefing, a chore that required a certain disconnection by the viewer lest he or she go comatose.

Some time passed as Remmick stared at the vacation schedule, trying to be Solomon, juggling people's names, marking them as VAC or IN, a perverse wielding of power he neither sought nor enjoyed. At one point-- it could have been 20 minutes or two hours later-- he got up for a change of scenery and walked to his office door to stare out at the newsroom. The seat occupied by the young woman named Gwen was now filled by Hilde.

Remmick walked over and soon came to see a bandage over the bridge of her nose and a smaller one on her left cheek just under her eye, partially covering a bruise.

"Holy shit," he said on his approach. "What happened to you?"

She looked up at him briefly but returned immediately to her screen, apparently rapt by the daily Pentagon briefing. She was typing madly-- deployment of reserves through the first quarter of 2009-- ENTER.

Remmick turned and walked back to his office, trying not to wonder too much. He sat down heavily in his creaky chair and stared at the number two monitor which showed Kaleidoscope's air. The sound was off. He was trying to read anchor Alan Parkman's lips.

One second, he was looking down at some paperwork sitting on his desk. The next second, his door suddenly closed and Hilde sat in the chair against the wall at a 90 degree angle to him. He was actually startled by her sudden appearance.

"Hey," he said.

She stared straight ahead for a while, then bowed her head.

"I said no," she said in a small voice.

"No to what?"

"No to Ronald."

Remmick looked more closely at the bruise under her eye, wicked and purple, blotched onto the perfect canvas that was her face.

"And he did that?" he asked, pointing.

She nodded almost imperceptibly. "At my place, last night. I told him I didn't want to anymore and he could tell whoever he wanted about me."

She slowly raised her eyes to Remmick's, her chin aquiver and tears welling up.

"But he didn't care," she started to sob quietly. "He said he owned me and he would never go back to life without me."

Remmick didn't say a word. He believed it all too easily.

"When I got up and told him to get out of my apartment, he whipped around and backhanded me." Her tears flowed freely. "I think I went halfway across the room, knocked against the glass coffee table on the way down."

Remmick urgently wanted to go to her, but he resisted.

"He said I had it coming. He said he just wanted to love me and how could I do this to him. I couldn't talk, I was totally shocked. I couldn't get off the floor." She touched her cheek and winced. "Then he just left."

"Did you call the cops?" Remmick asked.

She shook her head.

"Why the fuck not?"

"I drove myself to St. Luke's emergency room, told them I fell," she said wanly. "I went back home and took a shower and went to bed."

Remmick knelt down on the floor in front of her to look into her eyes without making her raise her head.

"You should have stayed home," he said. "Go home now."

She looked at him with steely eyes, which she wiped dry. She took a breath, straightened herself out and spoke in a monotone.

"I want him to see me," she said. "I want him to know I'm here."

"You can't keep playing this game with him," Remmick said. "These guys don't back off, Hild. They get more and more violent."

"He was right," she added. "I did have it coming. I should never have let it get this far."

"Are you out of your fucking mind? You're the victim here. If you had called the cops right away, they probably would have gone to his house and arrested him on the spot."

"His word against mine," she said softly.

"No. You have bruises; the cops have to arrest him. It's considered domestic violence."

"Oh, wouldn't that be a hoot," she spat bitterly. "A domestic, for Christ sake."

She stood up and straightened her clothes, wiped away a last tear. Remmick stood up. They were face to face.

"Don't say a god dam thing, Bud. I swear to god--"

He said nothing as she opened the door and walked out. She went back to her desk, donned her headphones and began looking at the next event on her screen.

That night, Remmick sat with Maggie on the porch at dusk, a citronella candle on the bench and a light breeze filling the air. It was fall but still warm enough to sit outside. She had wine and seltzer. Remmick had Absolut on the rocks.

"She doesn't want me to do anything," he said.

"Then, you can't do anything," came her response.

"I think she's all alone, Mag."

"Maybe," she answered, "and that would be her choice."

"It's fucking sexual harassment. It's assault, for Christ sake."

"It's her deal."

He looked at her hard.

"What?" she asked.

"I guess I expected a little more sympathy," he said flatly.

She took a swig of her drink, then looked out to the street.

"It was never enough for you to be a boss," she finally offered. "You need to be everyone's friend, too. You're stuck in between."

As usual, Remmick knew she was right. It was irritating.

"Sucks for me," he mumbled.

"Sucks for her," she corrected.

By going to prison, Remmick traded one claustrophobic world for another. His tiny office and small circle of employees and friends were supplanted by a tiny cell and a new, small circle of, well, cons. In fact, he reasoned, his job at Kaleidoscope prepared him, in a way, for jail. At the time, he never regarded his office as a cell, but now the parallels were staggeringly clear-- confined space with little opportunity for escape; limited contact with the outside world; a cabal of codependents; nothing but bad news incoming; a sociopath in charge.

Remmick's lawyer, Arnie Shapiro, thought the irony was quite delicious.

"It was meant to be," he loved to say in his Darth Vader voice. "You have fulfilled your destiny."

Arnie relentlessly looked at the bright side of things. It really made Remmick sick.

"Another year or so and you'll be out on parole, Bud," he told him on his last visit. "This was definitely the right path."

"Please inform my wife," Remmick responded. "I'm not sure she's on the same path anymore."

"Ah, don't worry, man. I've seen it a million times. The first year or two are hard, but they settle in."

"A million times?" Remmick questioned.

"Well, maybe not a million."

"They settle in? You've seen this before?"

"Fuck, yeah. It's always harder on the spouses. They have to deal with the real world shit."

"Tell me about it."

"Let me guess," he said, repositioning himself in his metal chair and staring off, reaching for a cloud. "The steely eyed determination so present during the pre-trial period was absent. Her wandering gaze betrayed her desperation. Her former strength was replaced by anger. Finally, the tears flowed and she questioned motives that were previously held as pure. She rose from the table and offered a kiss with no heart, no soul, perhaps not even love, leaving him sitting there alone at the cold, metal table."

Remmick was appalled and amused all at once.

"Nice, huh?" Arnie said with an idiotic grin. "From my book."

"Oh, great," Remmick said, rolling my eyes. "Your book."

"Don't worry, the names will be changed to protect the innocent," he said, pausing to look Remmick straight in the eye, "and the guilty."

It stung. Remmick said nothing for a while. Then: "Do you have anything constructive to tell me?"

Arnie was still on his pink cloud, but the pregnant silence finally caught up to him.

"Um, well," he began, "the super was none too pleased with your parole hearing report."

"Fuck him."

Arnie responded with a cold stare and, "Alrighty." He stood and thrust his hands into the pockets of his navy, pinstriped trousers. "So, this is how it'll be, then?"

"How what will be, counselor?"

"The next year. Piles of shit in your cell? Beating off in front of guards? Being a douche bag to the CO's? The CO's, man, they can be your best friends here, you know."

"You sound just like my wife," Remmick said, irritated again.

"I see," Arnie answered with a small nod. Then he leaned close to say, "I bet that CO over there would let you fuck me in the corner. You know, if Maggie won't anymore."

Arnie thought this was hysterical and cackled like a witch. Remmick just stared at him.

"Or," he said through that stupid grin, "is your swell roomie already taking care of you?"

"My cellmate is swell and no, there's none of that going on," Remmick quickly responded. "And by the way, Arnie, fuck you."

The tone of those two words erased Arnie's grin and he became a lawyer again. He moved closer to his client, almost whispering in his ear.

"Bottom line, man, you can make the next few years as difficult or as easy as you want. You can go ahead and be pissed off at the world and make everyone around you pissed off and miserable in the process. Or--"

He stopped when he saw Remmick roll his eyes and shake his head.

"Never mind," he said tersely. "Bud knows best."

He reached under the table for his briefcase, pulled on his jacket, straightened himself out and turned towards the door. Before walking through, he turned and said over his shoulder, "When life in Bud Land starts getting old, call me. Until then--"

He stopped in midsentence and stood formulating something, finally raising his finger to punctuate the last word.

"--fuck you."

###

Chapter 5

A week after Hilde revealed the true nature of her relationship with Ronald Morone, Remmick got called to his office. It came out of the blue.

The office smelled clean and bleachy as Remmick walked in. Morone's monitors were on and his desk had the same, sparse accoutrements as the last time Remmick visited. Morone's little boy haircut was freshly gelled and his skin was as white and gooey as always.

"Have a seat," he said, gesturing to the one other chair in the room.

Remmick sat down. There was no immediate move to close the door, so Remmick guessed he wasn't going to be fired today.

"I'm going to be out of the office for a week, traveling," Morone said, actually looking at Remmick. "I want you to be in charge."

Remmick looked at him a little bewildered and managed, "OK".

"You're the only one out there who seems to know his ass from a hole in the ground."

It didn't seem like a statement that deserved a thank you.

"Thank you," Remmick said.

"Just do what you normally do, news wise. Message me on anything big, but if you need to make an instant decision, make it."

"I appreciate your confidence," Remmick managed.

Morone gave a small, absent minded nod while shuffling through stuff on his desk.

"You're married, right?" came a query Remmick wasn't expecting.

"Yes."

He looked at Remmick a little sideways, a look he couldn't figure out.

"Ever think about fucking someone else?"

It was said blasé and with no emotion, as though he was asking about Remmick's favorite color.

"Um, have I ever thought about it?"

"Uh huh," he answered, obviously waiting for an answer. Remmick shifted uneasily in the hard, plastic chair.

"That's an unusual question," is all he could come up with.

"Have you?" His persistence was unnerving and Remmick couldn't imagine what he was going for.

"Well, I guess I'd be lying if I said I never thought about it. Why?"

Remmick wasn't sure this was the right answer. Morone looked straight at him.

"Well, if you ever decide to do more than just think about it," he said, "have I got a girl for you." He continued staring straight at Remmick with a tiny nod and a thin-lipped smile that gave him a chill.

"Thanks. I'll remember that."

"What happens in Vegas stays in Vegas, right," Morone asked with eyebrows raised and yet another variety of cold, creepy smile.

"Sure," Remmick agreed.

As though a switch in his misshapen brain had suddenly been turned off, Morone immediately lowered his head again and returned to shuffling papers.

"You can go," were his final words.

And Remmick rose to get the fuck out of there.

###

Two days later, Remmick was sitting at home in the den watching a Seinfeld rerun. He remembered glancing at the time on the cable box-- 7:43pm. The phone rang and as usual, he wasn't eager to answer. Thank goodness for caller ID.

Maggie peeked at the display. "It's work."

Great, thought Remmick. And I'm in charge.

She handed him the phone and he hit the TALK button.

"Hello."

"Bud, it's Nate." He was the night assignment desk manager.

"Hey."

"Has anyone else called you yet?"

"You mean from work? No. Why?"

A slight pause was followed by the words, "Hilde Schimmel is dead."

Remmick's breath left him at once and he actually took a step backwards.

"What?"

"Hilde Schimmel is dead."

The color drained from Remmick's face and he forgot to breathe.

"What? When?"

"Her mother called," Nate said. "Took all her Oxycontin at once, about 30 pills."

"Oh--"

"Went to the hospital by ambulance. Never woke up."

"--god."

"Jesus Christ, Bud."

"Anyone call Morone?" he managed.

"No. I just got the call and I called you first."

"I'll find him," Remmick said as a cauldron of emotions began to bubble.

"Pretty fucking awful, huh?"

"Yea," he responded.

Remmick pushed END CALL and stared at the wall where the phone's charger was mounted. Flashes of dark light popped in his head and his breathing quickened. The hand clutching the phone clenched it tighter, suddenly slamming it onto its charger, almost pulling if right off the wall. As though watching someone else's actions, he saw that same hand make a fist and smash through the glass of a picture frame hanging right above the phone. A word shot out of his mouth, stabbing the still air.

"No!"

He stood tight and hurt and wanting to hurt someone. He was breathing hard and his hand throbbed. His face and forehead were damp. He took a step towards the kitchen and let out a moan, then quickly made it to the sink and vomited. Maggie appeared there, looking at a madman. She looked scared. She stared at him. She looked at the broken glass. She looked back at him.

"Hilde killed herself," Remmick said, thinly.

Her face changed immediately, softening. She came to him and slowly put her arms around him. He grabbed her arms and held her close.

They stood like that for a long time.

###

Chapter 6

Eating meals in the prison cafeteria was as surreal as it gets-- several hundred men all dressed exactly the same, standing in a slow-moving line, waiting for smackdowns of brown, dark green and beige mounds on an aluminum tray. CO's were stationed at strategic spots. Remmick liked to imagine they were guarding the food. The scene was repeated day in and day out.

All the inmates sat in the same spots each day. Levon and Remmick sat in the fourth and fifth seats in from the north end of the 15th table from the main entrance.

In his first 370 days of incarceration at King's Point, Remmick had never witnessed any insurrection in the cafeteria. The food was no worse than any he had had at school or at any other cafeteria. The inmates mostly ignored the unarmed CO's who mingled, though occasionally eyes did dart above to the CO's looking down from the mezzanine. They wielded assault rifles. It appeared that the cafeteria was neutral territory and that anyone with a problem seemed to leave it outside.

While Levon sat next to Remmick, he often spoke loudly to the group of black inmates who sat farther down the table from them, shouting across Remmick and over his food. At those moments, Remmick paused his eating and leaned back, waiting for Levon to finish.

"Whatsa matter?" Levon would always ask.

"I want to give you plenty of space to shout at those guys," was Remmick's response, or something similar.

"I gotta keep in touch," he would say.

"OK," Remmick would say, "but you're spitting on my food."

Levon would always chuckle at this, either because he was amused that he spit on Remmick's food or because the circumstance and conversation happened over and over again in the course of a week.

"I have a question," Remmick said, dropping his fork onto the metal tray.

"Send it," Levon responded.

"Do you ever re-think whether she deserved it?"

"Who?" responded Levon, paying attention to what appeared to be meatloaf. "My wife?"

"Yes."

At this he grinned. "I told you, man, that was an accident."

At this, Remmick grinned. "Yes, of course." He looked down at the remains of his meal, then back at his cellie. "As I said: do you ever re-think whether she deserved it?"

Levon placed a final fork full into his mouth, then placed the fork onto the tray. He picked up the paper napkin and wiped his mouth. He looked at Remmick.

"You know the most important thing I learned in AA?" he asked.

"No. What?"

"To have the serenity to accept the things I cannot change," he said with confidence. "Everything happens for a reason, my friend."

Remmick wasn't familiar with AA dogma but this sounded like a bastardization.

"You're not answering my question," Remmick persisted. "OK, let's say it was meant to be and it happened because it was supposed to and it was out of your control, etcetera. The question is simply, did she deserve it?"

Levon turned away from him at that point and looked down at the metal table, his grin unchanged.

"That's a question for my Higher Power," he said evenly, "and I don't believe I've heard the answer yet."

Remmick returned to his own meat loaf and imagined at that moment that he was eating the remains of Ronald Morone.

There was a funeral for Hilde Schimmel. It was held at the funeral home, probably because Hilde didn't go to church and didn't care much about god. At least, that's what she once told Remmick.

Everyone from Kaleidoscope came except Ronald Morone.

"You never really know what's in someone's mind, do you?" offered Amy Mellisch, another producer who was friendlier than most with Hilde.

In a chair at the front of the casket sat Hilde's mother, a frail woman, perhaps in her 80's, whose visage defined human devastation. Hilde once told Remmick the only person she had left who really cared about her was her mother. He'd assumed she meant left in her family. It looked like she was right.

Maggie and Remmick had offered the mother their condolences and stood at the end of an impromptu line of mourners trying to leave. Amy Mellisch was behind them.

"Such a god dam awful end," she said quietly.

"Yea," Remmick responded without emotion.

"Fucking boyfriend beating her up," she continued, "on top of her mom being sick and all."

"Hm?" Remmick grunted.

"She told me once her boyfriend occasionally wailed on her."

"Jeez."

"Yea. Well, guess he's not here today, though she never mentioned his name or anything so I really wouldn't know if he was here."

Maggie gripped her husband's arm tightly and led him out of the place at a slightly quicker pace than before.

Remmick lay awake for what seemed like hours that night. His stomach hurt. Hilde died and that was it. Life would continue as though her absence was insignificant. Why couldn't she pick up a phone and call someone before taking those pills? Why couldn't Morone back off? Why was pure evil allowed to thrive?

Remmick brought that stomach ache with him to prison since none of those questions was ever answered.

###

Chapter 7

Two days after Hilde Schimmel's funeral, it was freezing cold and snowy. Remmick remembered eyeing up the bank thermometer outside the Kaleidoscope building-- 23°F, 9:13AM.

He walked the 50-yards of hallway towards the newsroom, stopping along the way at the cafeteria. He approached the coffee machine. The word coffee was a cruel hoax. He inserted two quarters and the machine grunted and made a lot of noise and took forever to make a tiny cup of product, artificially lightened and over-sweetened. When it finally stopped, the cup was filled to the absolute top.

Remmick grabbed the cup and the boiling hot liquid spilled onto his thumb and forefinger. Next to the coffee machine was the snack machine, which contained a wide assortment of foods that were bad for you including Yodels. He readied a dollar bill, then rethought the idea as he caught a look at himself in the polished, metal facade of the machine. His gaze locked on the bulge that hung over his belt. He kept on walking, carefully holding his scalding hot, machine-coffee.

He had been settled at his desk with his ersatz coffee and New York Times when a commotion suddenly came from the corner of the room where the studio and control room were. There was yelling. Not surprisingly, Terry Crowder's voice punched through like a shrill siren.

"I did SO give the fucking wrap cue," came Crowder's voice

"You didn't give shit," came another voice Remmick recognized.

"I gave him a one minute cue! I gave him 30-seconds. I gave him 15, then wrap. Fuck if I didn't give him a wrap!"

Crowder was wide-eyed and nearly hysterical, the way he got when he knew he was right, but nobody believed him. He was having it out with director Chuck O'Brien, the man from whom Crowder took his orders each day and the man from whom Crowder was to take time cues and deliver them to the floor director over his headset. O'Brien was getting impatient with Crowder's intractability.

"Yea, I heard you say 15 seconds but I didn't hear the magic word WRAP! And because I didn't hear the magic fucking word, the weatherman didn't get the magic fucking cue, which meant he kept talking and made us run over!"

The weatherman, smooth as silk on air, reverted to his street persona, right off the corner of 20th and Columbia, when his ire got up.

"I didn't get a fucking wrap cue, man."

The floor director, a timid young woman, spoke up.

"Terry, I'm sorry but you didn't tell me to wrap him. You stopped giving cues at 15 and, well," she paused to inhale, "I'm not a mind reader."

"Deaf bitch! And you, Einstein," he yelled, holding a fist up into the weatherman's face. "If she holds up a fist, doesn't that mean you have 15 seconds to shut up? Doesn't that mean in 15 seconds, shut the fuck up?"

"Hey man, I didn't get no wrap cue," the weatherman responded, unmoved. "If I don't get no wrap cue, I keep talking. That's my rule. That's my fucking rule, man. How do I know you don't want me to keep talking? I don't get no wrap cue and maybe I think Parkman dropped dead of a heart attack and I gotta fill until he sits up again. I don't wrap if I don't get no mother fucking wrap cue. You got that, my man?"

"I'm not your man, you stupid pretty boy. You don't know Fuck One about being in front of a camera."

"And you don't know how to give wrap cues, yo."

Crowder was spitting words. "I spent an hour shoveling my god dam driveway and I drove through an unplowed fucking street and I listened to producers whine all fucking morning. Then, YOU don't know how to take a wrap cue."

The weatherman shook his head, unswerving and calmly reiterated, "Didn't get no wrap cue."

Crowder finally started walking away with his chin tucked into his chest, muttering under his breath.

And it was only 9:30.

The crowd dispersed into the low buzz of the newsroom. The feeling was different, and the sounds muted. Remmick retreated back to his office to stare at schedules. In the quiet of his little room, he suddenly felt overwhelming sadness. He stared at nothing, trying to touch the feeling. It was more an emptiness, a hollow gray cavern radiating incongruous warmth, maybe something trying to surface. It was annoying. Remmick decided to get up and take a walk, feeling suddenly like he wanted to cry.

###

He never ever went to the Kaleidoscope research library. He knew it existed and where it was. But Google had long ago replaced Dewey Decimal as the search engine of choice for him. Remmick saw the library as a place that might offer solitude and quiet and, frankly, a place to hide for a while.

It was on the first floor, a right instead of a left off the elevator, then another hard right into a corridor that led to a part of the broadcast center where he seldom ventured. There was a LIBRARY sign with an arrow pointing in the direction he was walking. It was a narrow little hallway, almost like a passageway to a secret cavern except carpeted and illuminated with track lights. After a trek of about 30 feet, another LIBRARY sign hung from the ceiling with an arrow pointing to a glass door on the right. Remmick stopped at the door which had a LIBRARY sign taped onto the glass from the inside.

Pushing through the door, he had to allow his eyes to adjust to the fluorescents. The lights hung about a foot from the ceiling, which had been painted white a long time ago but which was now devoid of any color at all. It gave the room the feeling of having no top. Under his feet, the carpeting matched the stuff in the narrow hallway. It smelled new. Behind a counter to his right stood a young woman neatly dressed in a pert, unrevealing, pale blue, buttoned top. She was in front of a computer monitor, tapping away at the keyboard. She looked up and said earnestly, "Good morning. Can I help you?"

"Um," Remmick daftly uttered, looking around. "Where is the Times archives?"

"Straight back," she answered without hesitation, pointing along the path he was taking. "It'll say newspaper archives. There are several computers. Just sit down at one, double click the NYT icon and you're off!"

She had walked from behind the counter revealing ironed blue jeans and brown Kangaroos. As she pointed down the aisle, she looked like an ad for White Girl magazine.

"Thank you," Remmick babbled lamely, and continued walking.

The library was quiet except for some distant shuffling and the occasional, faint crackle of a fluorescent bulb. Long metal tables with chairs neatly arranged around them greeted the arriving library customer, weakly inviting one to sit and read. Remmick walked past the tables along the small aisle which now became lined with large shelving units on either side. The shelving units where tall and narrow, wide enough only to hold a row of books front and back, and set on wheels which sat on a track embedded into the floor. These shelves created narrow aisles down which you would venture to find your book.

Remmick looked down one aisle and found a small woman squeezed in between two massive shelves that had rolled too close to each other. The shelving units at her front and back were right on top of her.

"Hang on," he offered and put both hands on the forward shelving unit and began to push. Its wheels creaked along the rusted and unoiled track. He pushed hard and for a moment it felt as though the top-heavy, book-loaded shelving unit would topple over onto the one in front of it. He eased off and then started again, placing his hands at a lower spot. The unit moved reluctantly, about eight inches, enough to give the woman a bit more room to maneuver.

"Thank you so much," she said.

"No problem."

As Remmick walked away, he gazed up and saw that the shelves rose well above his height, maybe eight or ten feet tall. There were dozens of the hulking, wheeled units making up the stacks of the library. He figured that to work here, one had to have decent upper body strength to roll these things back and forth carefully enough not to cause them to topple.

He saw the sign described by Ms. Perky and walked towards it to find another long table. This one had three computers sitting on its surface and three chairs positioned accordingly. All were vacant.

He chose the one at the far right, keeping the center seat as a buffer in case someone else sat down, the same way he chose in the men's room.

The moment he sat down, he caught a glimpse of a person standing between two shelves directly in front of him, but didn't take time out to look more closely. He was fixated on his computer, which had already begun racing through its hard drive to find the New York Times published on his birthday. A blinking bar announced it was SEARCHING.

Remmick sat back to wait and looked up over the monitor and found myself staring right at the figure standing between the two shelves. He was holding what looked like a magazine, reading it.

Remmick lost a breath. He felt an instant wave of nausea. His eyes squinted involuntarily at the sensation that draped over him like a blanket. He thought he heard a word escape but it wasn't a word. There was a loud pounding in his head that he could hear. His thoughts started to scramble and random feelings fought for dominance until one surged to the top.

Remmick's eyes were locked on the figure standing there, motionless, reading. He looked like any other man standing in the library, poring over a periodical, maybe smelling the glossy pages. He moved only enough to turn a page, then returned to his stance.

Remmick glanced back at his computer screen and saw the January 16, 1961, front page of the New York Times staring back at him. Why did he want to see that? He couldn't remember. He looked back up over his monitor and Ronald Morone had not moved an inch, absorbed by his copious reading.

Remmick thought he would leave his seat and try to see what Morone was reading. What could the pig possibly be so interested in, he wondered. Why couldn't he just stay wherever the fuck he belonged?

Remmick wouldn't give him the option of striking up a conversation, acting like they were pals, being oblivious to the loss the newsroom had just suffered. Remmick would not grant tacit approval of his criminal treatment of Hilde. In Remmick's mind, Morone stood as a gross deformity, a chunk of matter too base to be as highly regarded as shit. If I could step on him anonymously and walk away, Remmick thought, I would. He felt an ill-defined imperative to do something.

He rose and quietly disappeared into the shelves behind Morone. He got close enough to see what publications were on the shelf in front of him. He should have guessed-- Congressional Quarterly. He slipped into the aisle just behind him, the shelving unit that stood at his back forming a barrier between them. Remmick stood there for a moment, not thinking anything. He could smell Morone's scent-- rubbing alcohol, perhaps hand sanitizer or a wet wipe.

Remmick walked to the far end of his aisle and turned left, walking to the second to last aisle. There were now seven shelving units between Morone and him. He felt a knot in his stomach that had been getting tighter and tighter, a ball of fury gathering energy. He caught his breath for a moment and felt actual pain in his gut. It was overtaking his torso as his muscles tightened.

Hilde's face, tears streaming down, came to him. Her anguish, her desperation hovered in the air next to him. He could almost smell her. Then, that alcohol smell again.

His body suddenly lunged against the shelf, all 270 pounds landing square against the neatly boxed, 2002 editions of Time, Newsweek and U.S. News. Remmick's hands rose to brace against the shelf, evidently pushing it with even more force, sending the unit teetering on the floor track.

What was happening?

Remmick felt a strain somewhere, pain in his upper arms and his thighs. His head rested against the shelving unit as his hands pushed and his body heaved against it.

His hands pushed and his body braced and the 10-foot tall, book-loaded shelving unit slowly tipped over, the tiny back wheels leaving the track and raising into the air. It was moving by itself, the heavy unit pivoting forward on its front wheels and striking the unit in front of it. Now, all the wheels were off the floor as the entire shelf toppled forward onto the one in front of it, which then sent the next shelf toppling, then the next, then the next, then the next then the next in a sickening, predictable domino effect. It raised ungodly metal on metal sounds, rust scraping off surfaces and unoiled parts slashing together as hundreds of books and magazines slipped off shelves and onto each other and the floor. A loud, deep WHOOSH, followed by a horrifying crash ripped through the quiet in room. No human sounds emanated. Those sitting in the company cafeteria on the floor below reported feeling an earthquake.

Remmick watched it like a slow motion replay of a scene in a black comedy but it must have all been over in just seconds. Even after the movement stopped and the shelves lay toppled in an almost comical scene from a B disaster film, the echo of the roar resonated for a few more seconds. Remmick desperately hoped to wake up now.

He looked down at the floor and saw the bottom edge of the shelf in front of him tilted up about 60 degrees. The shelf had pushed the others over, giant dominoes that fell because just one was toppled. Books and magazines lay everywhere. Somewhere near the entrance was a woman's urgent voice. Remmick was waiting to wake up. He remembered he was at the Kaleidoscope library, sitting at a computer, when he saw him. Yes, Remmick started remembering that he came over here and sneaked around the shelves. Now, he was standing in this spot, frozen in a bad dream, struggling to wake up.

"Sir, are you alright?"

Remmick looked at the young woman who was trying to talk to him.

"Sir?"

"What?" he snapped.

"Are you alright?"

Remmick was standing and apparently uninjured.

"Of course," he said blankly. "Why wouldn't I be?"

She looked at him as though he were insane.

"Why don't you have a seat," she said shakily, gesturing to one of the three chairs at the computer table.

Remmick sat down at the same chair he was in earlier. The computer screen still had a newspaper page displayed. He stared at it, then slowly moved his eyes up to peek over the monitor. Where Morone had been standing, there was an absurdly horrifying scene- - library shelves leaning against each other at steep angles like toppled Jenga blocks and a jumble of books and magazines in haphazard piles and a translucent dust cloud swirling about. His eyes traveled over each protruding piece of metal, wooden support, each book back, magazine masthead and uprooted floor track, searching for the next catastrophic sight. They rested on an object that made his heart stop-- a brown shoe. It was standing on its heel seeming to defy gravity, with the sole facing him. He bent his head to the side, dreading what the altered view would reveal. The shoe was attached to an ankle clothed in a tan sock.

A period of time went by which Remmick couldn't measure. He remained seated and was soon flanked by men in Kaleidoscope security uniforms and a couple other men in ties. Ms. Perky was several feet away, talking to police officers and pointing in Remmick's direction. The pain in his gut was gone. He smelled something bad and saw vomit on the floor next to him. His hands were folded in his lap as he stared at the devastation that would be seen later that day in video replayed over and over on Kaleidoscope's air, on TV's across America, on

Remmick's TV at home where his wife would be watching.

###

The Kaleidoscope security guards, the police, the paramedics, everyone was very nice. In the beginning he kept thinking this was about someone else. He accepted the handcuffs as routine. He didn't try to hide his face as he walked through the lobby and out the front door through the breathless gauntlet of shouting reporters and their photographers. The looks on their faces were like none he'd ever seen directed his way-- inspecting, accusing looks.

There was no disputing the facts. The young librarian saw it all. Two surveillance cameras saw it all. Remmick was unable to speak for a while. His beleaguered attorney had no idea what to say, so he said nothing.

The ride in the rear of the unmarked Crown Vic was quiet. It was just like in the movies where large men sit on either side of the handcuffed suspect in the back seat. Unlike a regular patrol car, this one had ample leg room, probably more in consideration of the large detectives than of the passenger.

Remmick was hanging on to the vague notion that he might still snap out of this dream at any moment. But by the time he was sitting in the interrogation room with Arnie and a detective named Mark, the dream quality had worn off.

###

It made the most sense to plead guilty and save everyone, mostly Maggie, the agony of a trial. Ronald Morone's widow, a cackling, 35 year old witch named Jean, was not pleased. She wanted Remmick fried, or at least jailed for life.

The widow Morone aside, the consensus seemed to be that Remmick's act was an impulsive one borne of stress and emotional loss and that since he had been cooperative, gave no one trouble and had no criminal record, he would be dealt with leniently.

Arnie was brilliant. He found a psychiatrist who submitted an affidavit swearing that Remmick was emotionally distraught and insane for the 23 minutes up to and including the incident. Arnie later regaled Remmick with tales of impassioned, in-chambers speeches to the judge concerning his character, his history as a good boss, his stability as a husband, blah, blah, blah. Remmick had no choice but to thank him profusely over and over and call him the greatest lawyer since Johnny Cochran.

The sentence was a gift-- four years of jail time. Four years for killing a maggot of a man. Remmick was almost giddy.

At the sentencing hearing, the judge said he was a little troubled by the nature of the confession.

"You agree you caused the heavy shelves to fall onto Mr. Morone but you claim not to have any memory of it," he said. "You can see, Mr. Remmick, why this rings a bit disingenuous, can't you?"

Remmick remained silent. Arnie did the talking.

"Your honor, I refer you to Exhibit 14, the sworn affidavit from Dr.--"

"Yes, yes, counselor, I get it," interrupted the judge, gesturing Arnie to sit back down.

Jean Morone gave her rambling, screechy victim statement to a hushed courtroom, her voice rising hysterically and then dropping off suddenly, a cycle that repeated several times. He peeked over at Maggie. She gave her husband the vaguest little nod.

The judge finally gaveled the proceedings to a close and Remmick was allowed a final kiss from his wife before being led away, hands cuffed behind him.

Chapter 8

Remmick checked off each prison day on a festive, Ardmore Christmas Shoppe calendar. Another three months had passed since his parole hearing for a total of one year and three months out of a four year sentence.

Several things had not occurred to him about being in jail. It never occurred to him that he'd be bored. It never occurred to him that he'd be claustrophobic. It never occurred to him that sharing a small space with a roommate 20 hours a day would be irritating.

Remmick read a lot, mostly books from the prison library. They were big on the classics.

The laptop went away after the 13th month because of an incident in another prison. He really missed it.

Maggie was only answering one out of every five or six of his letters now and he could tell her heart wasn't in it. She had received a cash infusion from his parents who felt some strange responsibility for what he had done, so the bills were getting paid. His parents disowned him.

Arnie stopped his regular visits. He came when Remmick asked for him, but he had stopped asking after the first year. Remmick owed him just shy of $113,000.

The smells of the prison were cloying-- cold dampness, urine and bleach. The food was predictable and bland, though not horrible. The prison library, where he had a so-called job, was quiet as a grave. No one ever came in-- it was just a storage room for books to be delivered cell to cell.

The occasional security alerts were amusing and diverting. They tossed cells randomly a couple times a week. They hit Remmick's once. No contraband, fortunately. The worst behavior problem he had heard about was an inmate in another wing who spit at a CO during an argument. There had not been a lock-down since he had arrived.

Conversations with Levon about any matters of substance were circular and unproductive. He was still unable to speak of his crime without a healthy dose of denial, so Remmick didn't feel like talking about his. Lately, though, it was on his mind constantly. He did spend an hour one day with the prison chaplain, a nice young man named Father Timmons, who was about half his age and couldn't have had a clue what it was even like to have a car payment. He was patient and kind and a great listener. But that conversation kept coming around to god and god's will and the hereafter and god's love and oh my god, Remmick thought, I am going to commit another crime!

People with time on their hands-- lots of time-- think too much. That was what Remmick told himself when, from time to time, he thought the unthinkable-- that Morone didn't deserve to die. Father Timmons asked him if he thought he was god and had the wisdom to decide who should live and who should die. Remmick told him it wasn't his intention to make Morone die, but didn't think Timmons believed him. And anyway, the moment he started in with the god talk, Remmick tuned him out.

Father Timmons visited from time to time and after a while finally caught on that Remmick wasn't particularly interested in what he was selling. But there was that one day.

Timmons and Remmick were to meet in the visitor's room that day. No one else was there. Remmick was sitting alone, staring off through the wired glass of the heavy door when he spotted him. The CO opened the door and Father Timmons walked in wearing jeans and a faded red, short sleeved polo shirt, the kind a nice, upstanding minister might buy at The Gap. He had what Remmick could only describe as a neutral look on his face. He made his way over to the metal table where Remmick was sitting with his hands in his lap, feet flat on the floor. Once, Remmick had tried to put his feet up on the table and the CO instantly corrected that.

Father Timmons sat down deliberately, quietly, on the metal chair across the table from the sole inmate in the room. He glanced first at Remmick's face, and then steadied his gaze onto the table between them. There were none of the facial twitches that usually signaled he was about to speak. Without moving his head, his eyes met Remmick and he spoke.

"What were you thinking at the exact moment you pushed yourself against that shelf?"

All Remmick could manage was, "What?"

Timmons' eyes never left Remmick's. "What were you thinking at that moment?"

After another moment to process, Remmick responded. "What's the difference?"

Timmons managed to breathe in slowly, and then exhale slowly while studying him.

"What were you thinking at that moment," he asked again, his voice still at a medium drone.

"What does this fucking have to do--"

Remmick made himself shut up. Father Timmons didn't flinch. He didn't move at all.

"So then," Timmons began quietly, "you can't answer that question?"

Remmick's eyes darted away. He was now staring at the metal table.

"You don't remember?" Timmons queried. Remmick said nothing. "You won't remember?"

"I think we're done here," Remmick snapped at him.

The priest's gaze softened ever so slightly. Remmick thought he saw the vaguest hint of a smile.

"Yes," Timmons agreed. "We are."

Father Timmons quietly stood, pushed the chair back under the table and walked toward the door. The CO opened it and out he walked, leaving Remmick alone again.

That night, Remmick told Levon about his chat with the good Father.

"You got a god phobia," Levon offered. "Seen it over and over again in AA."

"Oh, yea?"

"Yea. That's why many of us don't call it god. We call it our Higher Power."

"Same thing."

"No. After you grow up with one version of god drilled into your head by the stupid adults in your life, you need to break free. The very word god corrupts the concept."

"What concept?"

Levon looked at his cell mate earnestly. "The concept that there's something bigger than you out there, fool."

Remmick smiled. "Oh. So, that's the concept?"

Levon detected the contempt in Remmick's voice. "The concept is this, Mr. Bud-- you control almost nothing. The people, the circumstances, the events and outcomes in your life-- how much of them have you controlled?"

Remmick considered trying to formulate an answer.

"But," he continued, punching the word, "you do control two things--"

Remmick could hardly wait.

"--your own actions and your own words."

After another few seconds, he broke his gaze. It would be no fun for him any more since Remmick wasn't responding. So, he climbed up to his bunk and lay quietly for the rest of the night.

Remmick sat up on his and stared through the cell bars at the darkened image of the cell across the tier. He did that for quite a while, trying to remember what he was thinking as he pushed the heavy shelves down onto Ronald Morone.

###

A year and seven months into Remmick's incarceration, there was good news and bad news.

The good news was his medical eval was great. He had dropped down to about 210 pounds and was actually in decent physical shape. His BP was 126 over 76. His bloods were all nominal, even the lipids.

The bad news was delivered in person by Maggie during a regular visitation.

"I'm done," she said simply.

"You're done?"

"I'm done."

The words startled Remmick but the idea did not. Once again, he defaulted to his first instinct.

"Don't I get a say in this?"

She gave him a strange look and cocked her head slightly, then said incredulously. "Are you kidding?"

"No, I'm not kidding."

She shook her head and looked away for a moment, then back at him.

"Of course you have a say, Bud. You can say anything you want. I might even care about what you have to say. But it's not going change that the marriage is over. Arnie is drawing up the papers for us."

"Arnie is doing what?" he spat.

"Oh, spare me," she said quickly. "He's doing it for free, for Christ sake. You owe him over a hundred grand."

"We owe him over a hundred--"

"Not after we're divorced," she jumped in.

It was Remmick's turn to stare incredulously. "So, this is about money?"

She looked at him hard and never blinked.

"Yes, Bud, it's about money. It's about prison. It's about a dead man. It's about isolation. It's about being a fucking outcast in my own neighborhood. It's about losing my job. It's about losing my fucking LIFE."

She punched the last word, causing the CO to perk up and look over at them. Her hands were shaking.

Remmick's hands were in his lap. He had no feeling in them, or anywhere else.

"The worst thing, Bud, the worst thing?" she said, turning away, then turning back to him. "The worst thing is, you really don't get it. And I'm not sure you ever will."

He felt the blood draining from his head and life draining from the rest of him.

"So, I'm done," she repeated. "Don't try to contact me any more. I'll get a court order if I have to."

Maggie gathered up her things, stood up and pulled her coat back on.

He remained sitting and said only, "Please, don't."

She froze and, looking down at him said, "Grow the fuck up."

Maggie turned and walked away from the table. The CO opened the door and watched her walk out.

Remmick stared at her space.

###

Chapter 9

Standing at attention-- a deliberate stance which he struck for effect -- Bud Remmick inhaled through his nose, stared directly into the eyes of the man who stood before him and spat the words, "How about, you go fuck yourself?"

Into the air they went, round and round, until they spiraled down onto the head of the other guy in the room.

"Excuse me?" was the incredulous response.

Remmick scrunched his forehead and glared through slit eyes. "Excuse you? What part didn't you get?"

The prison superintendent stood not ten feet away from him. His mouth was open. There were words trying to get out.

Remmick rolled his eyes, took a deep breath, looked at him straight on and said, "How about, you go fuck yourself, cunt?"

The superintendent's look softened and a weird sort of recognition how appeared on his face. He actually seemed to relax and put his hands in his pockets.

"Do you feel better now?" he asked with a grin that infuriated Remmick.

Those words pulled the pin. Remmick whipped around and put his hands on the first thing they could find-- an antique lamp on the small table next to him. He grabbed the glass shade with one hand, yanked it hard to unplug it from the wall, and then tossed the whole lamp against a glass-enclosed cabinet that held plaques and trophies, just behind and to the right of where the superintendent was standing.

It was one, swift motion. The crash was terrible. Glass shards flew everywhere. Several plaques inside the cabinet fell to the base with loud and consecutive thuds. The superintendent ducked, then flinched as a piece of flying debris struck him. Almost simultaneously, his office door flew open and two COs with shotguns stood in the room. They were greeted by a corner of devastation and the two men standing stock still in the middle of the superintendent's office.

"What the fuck," came out of one of the COs mouths.

The superintendent held up his hand and quickly said, "It's alright."

Remmick eyed them up, paying special attention to their very large guns. He hadn't seen what the weapons looked like close up before now. He could smell the oil used to clean them.

Behind them, in the reception area of the office, a couple of women peered into the open door, trying to see what was happening. Another inmate was there, too, sitting on the couch, craning his neck.

It did feel good, Remmick noted to himself, to call the superintendent a cunt and to toss the lamp into the glass case. Moments later, however, Remmick did not feel good, recognizing he had ignited the equivalent of a tire fire.

"Inmate Remmick is unhappy," said the superintendent with forced calmness and a slightly shaky voice. "Please take him to A-SEG for a 30-day vacation."

The COs had each taken a hold of one arm as a third arrived and reapplied the cuffs and shackles that had earlier been removed. Remmick let them do their thing without making any movement and said nothing.

"Mr. Remmick," said the superintendent, taking a couple steps towards him. He inhaled deeply and looked down to formulate his words. Then he turned his eyes to Remmick's.

"I don't know all your issues," said the super evenly. "Your case file only has the rent-a-shrink's affidavit from your sentencing-- temporary insanity, some bullshit. But-- and I mean this in all sincerity-- I'd suggest that for the next 30 days, you think about not only what you did here, but what really made you do it. Anger like yours will destroy you. I know this."

Remmick stared straight ahead and said nothing.

"Considering your crime, your sentence was a gift," spat the jailer. "If you're interested in extending your stay here, keep it up. If not, get your head out of your ass and grow up."

He turned to the mess in the corner, then back to Remmick and the guards. "Get him the fuck out of here."

Administrative segregation is like living in a blank piece of paper. The cells are tiny and contain the following: stainless steel sink, stainless steel toilet, concrete slab covered by a 1-inch thick mattress, a narrow window too high to look out of and a concrete protrusion from the wall next to the bed slab that acts as a kind of night table. Since the prison was fairly new, the walls were almost clean and the mattress still had some of its insides. It all smelled like bleach.

Remmick had been there for some hours. It got dark. Then, it got light again. At one point during the light time, a tray of food was pushed in through the slot in the door. At another point, the door actually opened and two COs stood there, shoulder to shoulder. One of them said, "Exercise." They shackled and cuffed him and helped him shuffle to a small, fenced in pen where he was to "exercise" for exactly one hour. He measured the dimensions by pacing them off--32 paces by 16 paces. He walked the perimeter several times, sat in a corner, and then walked the perimeter again. The heavy door opened and the same two COs appeared again carrying the familiar shackles. They re-applied everything and walked him back to the small cell. The door closed and he stood next to the concrete bed again.

Remmick looked around as though there were actually things to look at. He shuffled back to the thin mattress on the hard concrete slab and sat down. There was a faint sound in the distance of, maybe, a power generator or motor. Here where he sat, there was no noise except his own breathing.

There were many days Remmick was grateful for his bed in his modest suburban home. The comforter, bunched up and cool under his nose and chin, shielded him from evil. The quiet outside the windows allowed his imagination to soar, from the sleepy cave of his dark room to the bright and sunny places where he ruled the world-- the newsroom, the driver's seat of his Beemer, the uncomplicated world of perfection and compliance he knew as Budland. In Budland, he was President, King and Chief Justice, editor in chief of the one and only newspaper and

Vice President and General Manager of the one and only television station. Traffic stopped when he approached in his Beemer from the driveway or intersection, allowing him unfettered access to the lane of his choice. Traffic laws were maintained by meticulous police trained at the Budland Police Academy and given unchallenged power to administer justice on the spot. A favorite scenario was the Left Turn Mother Fucker who sat at a red light, waiting to make a left turn in front of the on-coming traffic which had the right of way. As the light just turned green, the Left Turn Mother Fucker hit the gas and hung his left turn in front of the opposing traffic which was now denied the right of way. As the Left Turn Mother Fucker sped away in his arrogance and ignorance, not one but two Budland Police Officers, who were right there and saw the whole thing, chased him briefly, pulled him over and got out of their cruisers. They would approach the front of the Left Turn Mother Fucker's Escalade, one shouting loudly at the driver through the driver's window, the other opening the passenger door to shout at him from that angle. Tickets totaling $10,300 would be issued and the officers would be laughing loudly as other motorists in Subarus and Chevys passed by slowly, giving the Left Turn Mother Fucker the finger.

The cushy feel of the comforter was absent, replaced by the neutral scratch of a polyester-blend blanket against his cheek. The perfectly firm Sealy Posturepedic gave way to a one-inch thick pad plopped onto cool concrete. The only thing similar to his old bedroom was the sneak of outside light that pushed its way in through the narrow window that was too high for him to look out of. It reminded him of the orange colored street lights on Wharton Lane, small snatches of which eked into his bedroom, even in the dead of night, to keep him company as Maggie snoozed next to him, oblivious to his middle-of-the-night fears. He wasn't sure where the light creeping into his isolation cell was coming from, but it reassured him in a familiar way and allowed him to sleep, night after night.

Daylight always arrived before Remmick awoke. He always forgot where he was for the first few moments, irritated at the hard surface that greeted him and the neck pain that resulted from a pillow evidently stuffed with tissue paper. There were always distant sounds--a motor, muted voices, someone elsewhere in A-SEG singing or talking to himself. He welcomed the sounds because they were all he had, except for his hour of exercise and meals. He occasionally allowed himself a chuckle at the memory of a conversation he and Maggie once had with Maggie's friend Loretta, a nurse at an assisted living residence in Union County, who said the old residents all looked forward to exercise, their three meals, then going back to sleep.

Sleeping was peaceful, once Remmick got to sleep. Waking was always a rude event heralded by the sound of the metal food tray being pushed through the slot in the door. There was no dawn or dusk, no dead of night or early evening, no mid-day or late morning. There was some light, more light, less light, over and over and over again.

The first night, Remmick etched a small check mark onto his solid concrete wall with a finger nail in an attempt to begin keeping track of the number of days. The next day, a CO entered the cell and headed straight for the wall next to the bed, obviously knowing what he was looking for.

"Put another mark on that wall and you'll earn another month in here," he said with an edge, then quickly left. The entire, one-way interaction took less than 45 seconds. Suddenly alone again, he said "fuck it" out loud and returned to a supine position on the cot.

After that first 24 hours, he lost track of time. He only knew dark and light, dark and light.

One morning, instead of hearing the food tray scrape across the floor, he heard the chunk of the lock and the clatter of the key turning the tumbler on his cell door. His eyes opened, fully expecting to be confronted by a dream. There stood a CO, shackles in hand, his partner behind him.

"Time to go home," said the CO with a stupid half grin.

Ha, good one.

###

Chapter 10

The former Margaret Schlossberg met her current husband in a TV newsroom. At the time, he was a hotshot assignment editor, she an intern who had taken five years to become a college senior. The attraction between them was not immediate, to say the least. He perceived her the way he did other interns--eager, but clueless. She perceived him as arrogant, cocky and dismissive. In later conversations, he admitted to being all three.

Margaret was raised in the Philadelphia suburb of Merion, a small town of old money, overgrown willow trees and diverse housing stock that ranged from four bedroom splits to million dollar mansions. She had fond memories of her home on Bala Avenue, a modest three bedroom crammed into a small lot and surrounded by similar homes. Her friendships were based on this geography and were later enhanced through her teenage years at Lower Merion High School, home of basketball star Kobe Bryant.

It was at Lower Merion that Margaret became Maggie. It happened the day Michael Jacobs called her Margie.

"Don't call me that," she quickly corrected him. "I hate that name."

"OK, Margie," continued Michael with a hyena laugh that was irritating.

"Don't call me Margie," she said more insistently.

"OK, Margie of Merion," he cackled. His face was scrunched in laughter and his eyes were slits as he almost doubled over until the sudden crack of wood on his head stopped him in his tracks.

"I said, don't call me Margie, dickhead," she said, still holding her wooden clog sandal in her right hand.

"Oww, what the fuck!" shouted Michael Jacobs.

"It's Maggie," she corrected him. "Maggie the Cat."

"Fine. Fucking Maggie the Cat," he babbled. "Jesus Christ!"

Little did either of them know they would remain friends through high school and beyond, he taking credit for the name Maggie The Cat as though he had discovered uranium.

There were times in college when Maggie thought she would never get married, even have a real boyfriend, though she was admired by almost every male she met. To her chagrin, she discovered that athletes and musicians were attracted to her, hoping she would become their weekend booty call. There was no instance in which any of the men who came on to her had any interest in 1) her opinions, 2) the world around them or 3) current events. It was sad and tedious, telling one after another that they were nice, but that they should fuck off. So, there was no expectation that anything would change at the TV station where she would do her internship.

But one day, the edgy assignment editor named Bud asked her a question.

"Do you date at all?" he asked.

"Not really," she answered.

"Oh," he said and went back to listening to his police scanner.

"I drink," she said after a few seconds of standing there.

He looked back at her. "We go to this place in Narberth called The Greeks after work sometimes."

"I know The Greeks," she said with a bit more animation. "I got thrown out a couple years ago for underage drinking."

"Well, that is charming, of course," said Remmick. "I presume you are at least 21 by now, yes?"

"Twenty-two, actually. I've been on the five-year plan at school."

Remmick grinned. "Whatever works. If you'd like to join us, no problem."

"I'll think about it," she said and resumed gathering scripts from the producer's out-bin.

Following a number of rendezvous at The Greeks and other watering holes, Remmick discovered Maggie Schlossberg was not, in fact, clueless. While she had a sharp tongue, she was well informed about the news, knew the local geography quite well and was friendly with several Lower Merion cops due to bad behavior on her part that was later forgiven, in no small measure, due to a winning smile, sparkling blue eyes and a charming command of boy-pleasing bullshit.

The night of their first kiss, she was surprised. They were leaving The Greek's and were about to part ways to their respective cars when they simultaneously stopped walking and he faced her and leaned in, planting it on her lips. It wasn't an obnoxious, lingering mess, just a sort of extended peck. Then, he pulled back to see her reaction.

"Oh my," she said. "To what do I owe that?"

He looked at her, annoyed. "I couldn't help myself. Was that wrong?"

She looked into his eyes and grinned, leaning in to another that lasted a few seconds longer. They separated again.

"I guess it wasn't wrong," he said softly after the second kiss.

"I like you," she said. "I don't know why because you are basically a geek."

"I know, and I'm too tall," he said, aware that he had to bend down significantly to get his lips to match up with hers. "Can you deal with it?"

"Obviously," she said as she took his hand and they walked to her car. They parted with one more kiss of the earlier variety. Remmick kept walking to where his car was parked.

Almost twenty years later, it was a day during which the sky was so blue and the air so clear, Maggie Remmick thought it was a mistake. How could it be such a perfect day, warm with still air, yet refreshing and clean?

She drove with her window open and her left elbow resting on the door. There wasn't much a 2004 Subaru Legacy sedan could do to stand out from the crowd, which was fine by her. She'd had a snoot-full of standing out.

She was stopped at the light at 8th Avenue and 52nd Street and folded down her visor to peer into the vanity mirror. Immediately, her eyes stared back at her, big and blue with tattered lashes and every small wrinkle around them magnified by the mirror which was about 7 inches from her face. The makeup was OK but there was only so much she could do about the pouches under her eyes. She blamed Bud for those. A few locks of her blond, curly, Shirley Temple mop hung into the picture as well. She whisked them away with her right hand which also held a cigarette. For that, she blamed no one but herself.

Still, she was a pretty good specimen at 41, she concluded. As long as she could cut herself loose from the nightmare that had been the last year, she would be fine.

The light turned green and she took her foot off the brake to allow the Subaru to ease into the movement of traffic. It took another ten minutes to travel the three blocks to 55th Street.

Sitting on a leather sofa, watching CNBC on a 42-inch flat screen and sipping an iced latte through a straw out of a Dunkin Donuts cup, Arnie Shapiro had most of the comforts of home in his office at 55th and 7th Avenue. He actually spent most of his time here, so why not?

Arnie's client list was stuck at one for a very long time following his graduation from Temple law school. His first client came upon him at McGlinchey's one night when he was sitting at the bar, watching the Phillies and Dodgers sweat one out at the Vet. The two guys standing behind him were speaking in loud voices. Arnie was sipping a beer pensively when he noticed the loud voices were actually angry voices. It was an argument about work or a contract or... something. Arnie was content to let them spit at each other. He tried tuning them out, sipping his beer, glancing at the television when suddenly the two of them bumped into him.

"You almost knocked this guy off his chair, asshole," said one pissed party to the other.

"Stop it," the other pissed party spat. "Stop that. Stop that."

"Stop what?" queried pissed party Number 1.

"You're con-dis-tending," answered Number 2 with the confidence of a drunk. "You fuck."

With the last words, #2 slumped against Arnie, literally pushing him off the bar stool, forcing Arnie to get to his feet quickly before ending up on the floor on his rear end.

"Whoa," said Arnie quickly. "Easy, boys."

"Who you calling boy?" challenged Number 2.

Arnie picked up the dish of pretzel mix sitting on the bar in a brown, plastic bowl, and shoved it at Number 2.

"Have some," he said with an inviting tone and a sincere, wide-eyed gape.

Number 2 straightened himself up and looked at the bowl, reaching in and grabbing a couple pretzels and cheese twists and shoving them into his mouth immediately.

Number 1 left without saying a word.

"Have a seat," said Arnie, guiding Number 2 to his bar stool.

The drunk's eyes were only half open at this point. He allowed himself to be placed on the stool.

"Thangyoo," he slurred, cocking his head and staring at himself in the mirror behind the bar. "I thing I just fired my lawyer."

"Oh, yea?" said Arnie.

Number 2 nodded at himself, his eyes blinking, body swaying ever so slightly.

"Gotta be in court tomorrow," he said weakly.

"How come?"

Number 2 raised his head and searched for his non-existent drink.

"Can I get another?" he shouted at the bartender.

"No, you can't," the bartender answered.

"Well, fuck you," he shouted at the bartender.

"Thank you and fuck you," the bartender answered with a lilt.

This pleased Number 2, who broke into a grin and propped up his chin with his right hand, elbow resting on the wet mahogany. "DWI. Again."

Arnie had to remember what the question was.

"So, now you need a lawyer?" he said.

"I don't need any fucking lawyer," Number 2 replied indignantly, and proceeded to vomit on the floor between his legs.

There was a brief clamor as the bartender called for someone from the kitchen to bring the mop. Arnie stepped aside as did several other patrons, all scrambling to avoid the puke.

The vomiting stopped after what seemed like an eternity of wet, followed by dry heaves, and Number 2 sat back down, wiping his mouth with his hand, then wiping his hand on his pants. He ran the same hand through his hair, gazing at the mirror again. There was a small glimmer of lucidity escaping the whites of his eyes.

"Yes, I now need a lawyer," he said.

Arnie looked at him, looked at his hands, then extended his.

"Arnold Shapiro," he said, grasping Number 2's unsteady hand, accepting its recent encounter. "Esquire."

Number 2 looked at him, not knowing what any of those words meant and said simply, "My name's Bud."

Four years later, Arnold Shapiro was lasered into a brushed nickel plate screwed onto a polished mahogany door, which led into a very nice ante room complete with very nice, soft carpet, a leather couch, glass coffee table, moderately expensive artwork by a former law school pal and a Samsung 42" LED television. On that television at the moment was Squawk Box on CNBC. Joe Kernan was interviewing the juvenile CEO of an upstart IT company that specialized in e-commerce security, encryption and other things Arnie could barely fathom. His mind wandered as the interview bogged down in the language of Wall Street insiders and it was actually good timing that his phone rang at that moment.

"Hi," he snapped into the phone.

"Margaret Remmick is here," said a female voice.

"OK, show her in."

Arnie hung up and immediately stood and faced his door. After about two seconds, the door swung open and Maggie Remmick walked in slowly.

"Maggie," said Arnie with the mock enthusiasm of a salesman. "So great to see you."

She extended her hand. "Hello, Arnie."

They shook briefly.

"Have a seat," he offered immediately.

She moved two steps towards a large, leather chair that was caddy-corner to his couch and sat down, placing her bag on the floor. Arnie sat down at the end of the couch closest to her chair.

"You're looking great," said Arnie, wide-eyed.

She looked at him for a moment and managed, "Thank you."

"I'm glad you came," he said with sudden sincerity.

"Why?" she asked with no emotion.

His toothy smile altered slightly as he attempted to understand the meaning of her one-word question.

"Uh, well..."

She stared at him.

"Because I know you've been in a state of limbo..."

She never flinched.

"... over your, um... life. You know, with Bud in prison, etcetera..."

She broke her stony gaze and said, "I'm not here because I want to be here, Arnie. I'm here to get a fucking divorce and I'm not all that happy about it, so I'd appreciate it if you knocked off the patronizing blather and just tell me what I have to do."

Arnie's face suddenly went blank, the smile disappeared and he became flustered.

"Oh sure, Maggie," he began with a return of his prior faux sincerity. "I can't even imagine how difficult this must be for you."

Her eyes finally turned away from him as she looked out the window over his shoulder. She saw the same bright, blue sky she noticed while driving to his office. She heard Arnie begin to speak again, but she wasn't listening. She thought of Bud Remmick, her husband, and what was once their life in that little house.

"...uncontested divorce. All you need is both parties to sign off."

Arnie continued speaking. She felt nauseous and tired and very, very sad.

"...divide up property and other assets... you know, whatever money there is."

It was the denial, maybe, she thought, Bud's failure to comprehend the big picture. It wasn't all about her, about money. She had really tried to come on board with the whole adventure scenario.

"...have this over in just a couple of months, Maggie. Maggie?"

She popped back to reality. Arnie was behind her chair, his right hand now resting on her right shoulder.

"This doesn't have to be the end of your life," said Arnie in a hushed tone, very close to her right ear. She could smell both his cologne and his staggeringly minty breath.

"Life goes on," he continued, his hand firmly in place, his lips inches from her ear. "And I'm here to help you through it."

In a conspiratorial tone that exactly matched his, Maggie said, hardly lifting her head, "Arnie, in my bag is a Swiss Army knife Bud gave me for my birthday two years ago. It has a really useful, miniature saw blade. I will use it to cut off your fucking hand if you don't move it right now."

Removing the hand immediately, Arnie stepped away from the back of her chair and walked around it, making his way now to his desk which was about ten feet across the room.

"No need for hostility, Mags," he said, raising his hands in a what-the-fuck stance. "I just want to make it clear that I am here to help you through any obstacles. You and Bud are friends."

This elicited a weak grin from Maggie. "Yes, of course," she said. "Are we friends enough to get a break on the cost of the divorce? I have, like, no money."

"Let's not worry about money now, Maggie," said Arnie in an almost-sincere tone. "I'm here to help."

"Sorry, Arnie, but I need to know now what it's going to cost. We're already into you for over 110K."

"Let's call it part of the package," he replied. "No additional charge for drawing up the papers, filing them and dealing with the court."

"Can I get that in writing?" she asked without hesitation.

He paused, looking a bit wounded, then nodded. "Of course."

Maggie grabbed her bag from the floor and stood. "Thank you, Arnie."

He walked out from behind the desk and came to her, taking her hand.

"Of course, Maggie," he said, gazing into her eyes. "It'll all be over soon."

She nodded slightly, then broke his gaze quickly and headed for the door.

"Any time you need to talk, about anything," he offered, letting it hang there.

She rolled her eyes before turning to answer him, then turned and quickly snapped them back into place.

"Thank you," she said and quickly slid out the door, closing it softly and deliberately behind her.

###

Chapter 11

Maggie had stopped coming to see Bud months ago. So, it was confusing at first when CO2 told him he had a visitor.

"Tell my lawyer I'm not interested," Remmick said.

CO2 approached the bars of the cell.

"Tell him yourself," he said. "And it's not your lawyer."

"Who is it?" Remmick asked. But CO2 walked away and was replaced by two other COs. One of them, a clean-cut, dark skinned boy with pretty blue eyes, stood close to the cell door as it opened. The COs motioned for Remmick to go with them.

Various faces from the outside world populated the visitors' room, many familiar to Remmick after all this time. As he walked in through the metal door, one person immediately caught his attention, a generic white man, sitting alone at a metal table with his hands folded, wearing jeans and a pale green polo shirt. The man, with a not-quite-buzz-cut and clear complexion, looked to be in his 20s and was looking straight at Remmick as he shuffled into the room.

The young, blue eyed CO gave a slight nod towards the mysterious visitor and Remmick understood. The COs left the room to a colleague who stood at the door, arms folded.

Remmick slowly walked towards the man whose gaze never broke with his. His head pivoted slightly as Remmick approached the table. The young man did not rise or offer his hand. He simply stared at Remmick for another few moments.

Remmick broke the staring contest first, taking a deep breath and looking away for a second or two, before turning his head back to his visitor to speak. But the young man beat him to it.

"You lost weight," he said without emotion. "You look the same, but skinnier."

"I know Arnie's pissed," responded Remmick, "but I didn't ask--"

"I don't know anyone named Arnie," interrupted the young man. "But I definitely feel like I know you."

Remmick became annoyed.

"Who the fuck are you?" he asked directly with twisted brow.

The man seemed unsure how to proceed. He eyed Remmick's face, scanning it for, something.

"Richard Morone," the man finally said without taking his eyes off Remmick's. "Ronald Morone's son."

Remmick stopped breathing. He felt the blood drain from his lower body and a sickening weakness.

"Damn," said the young man with a barely detectable grin. "So much for the poker face."

Remmick suddenly took a massively deep breath, finally realizing he hadn't been breathing. He was staring straight into the eyes of this young man.

"I saw you on TV a couple times back then," said the man calling himself Richard Morone. "I've heard TV makes you look fatter."

A son, yes. Remmick remembered now-- the Widow Morone's impassioned, hysterical statement at the sentencing.

"You're his son," Remmick said flatly. "You were mentioned at--"

"The sentencing, yes," said Richard. "I saw it on TV. Poor, stupid mommy."

It now occurred to Remmick to sit down and he did so, slowly.

"Uh," began Remmick. "What, what, um--"

"What am I doing here?" finished Richard.

Remmick nodded a little. "Uh huh," he managed. Remmick detected no anger. In fact, he was having trouble reading the man at all.

Richard folded his arms as if to close up, and then scratched his forearms with fingers of the opposite hands while looking into the table as though it were a piece of fine art.

Remmick waited for what seemed like forever for an answer to Richard's self-asked question.

"My father was a prick," the young man said finally, without passion, without looking up. "He beat the shit out of my mother for as long as I can remember. She just dealt with it. We dealt with it."

Remmick sat, quiet, staring.

"When I was away at college," Richard continued, "it apparently got much worse." He shifted in his chair, still lightly scratching his arms. "One night, she called me, barely coherent after a hall-of-famer. She could barely talk. I called the cops on him."

Remmick was mesmerized. Richard Morone's tone hardly changed but he looked somewhere into Remmick's face.

"He called me back, screaming and spitting into the phone, raging. I had ruined his life by calling the cops, see. Of course, I immediately felt guilty." He stopped there and fixed on Remmick's eyes. "Isn't that fucked?"

Remmick gave a small shrug. He was still wide eyed.

"I slept on it," Richard resumed quietly. "The next day, I decided I would never see either of them again."

Remmick watched Richard's face change now. There was a small smile.

"And then," Richard said, first smiling at the floor, then turning his eyes to Remmick's, "you killed him." There was no hysteria or anger, no judgment or acrimony, just a conclusion.

Remmick remained frozen, his eyes on Richard's.

"I had dreamed of killing him for years," Richard continued, his eyes searching the table top. "Really. I fantasized about how best to do it-- neat or bloody, poison, run him down with the car, whatever. The hate--"

He stopped, catching himself as he felt a tightening that was out of his control. His eyes rose from the table and met Remmick's again.

"And then, you pushed some stupid bookshelves onto him and snuffed him out," he said with wonder in his eyes. "Just like that." His face broke into an almost-giggle. "I couldn't believe it."

Remmick couldn't believe this entire conversation.

"I felt this overwhelming relief at first," said Richard. "Free at last, you know? But my mom, well, her reaction wasn't what I expected at all."

His face transformed, again.

"She cried and cried. She literally moaned about her Ronnie. Her Ronnie, for Christ sake. She was inconsolable. Some days, hysterical."

He shifted and looked down at the table again.

"I came home, finally," he continued. "And the person who was there wasn't my mom anymore. She took one look at me and I could see her change in that moment. She screamed at me for staying away, for calling the cops that night, screamed about you, screamed about the cops and Kaleidoscope and how the whole world ganged up on her Ronnie--"

His voice trailed off. His arms unfolded and his hands came to rest on his lap.

"Her Ronnie," he repeated. And, with an exasperated half smile and matching exhale, he added, "She loved him. She actually loved him. Man, that really fucked me up."

Remmick continued staring at Richard Morone, still processing. Dread had changed to something else.

"So, I simply said goodbye," he said. "Her response was, good riddance. From then on, I followed everything on television."

Remmick heard his own voice at that moment.

"I'm sorry," it announced, quietly.

Richard looked at him quizzically. "For what?"

Remmick stared into the young man's face.

There was silence between them for an immeasurable period. Remmick looked around the room. The CO had glanced at them but seemed unconcerned. There were other visits happening around them, hugs and kisses and hushed conversations between couples. And here was an island of hushed contemplation between two men sitting at a metal table.

"Why did you come?" asked Remmick.

Richard searched for the answer to that one.

"I know he must have done something," said Richard Morone. "Something to--"

"I'm not sure I should be talking about--"

"--deserve it."

Remmick rethought being on defense. He thought of words Maggie repeated many times during the months leading up to his incarceration: What could the truth hurt? Easy for her to say.

"I only worked for him about a year," said Remmick evenly. "I found out he was blackmailing an employee who had lied on her job application."

"Her?"

"Yes, a female. She never graduated from college. He called her on it. Then, he made her an offer to allow her to keep her job."

The young man was now the mesmerized party. "Yes?"

Remmick began to search for elegant, diplomatic words, manager words. It took too long.

"He was fucking her."

He watched for a reaction.

"He threatened to out her to the whole New York broadcasting industry so she couldn't work anywhere else if she told anyone. She came to work in tears many days."

Richard remained impassive and continued listening.

"She came to me, confided. I told her to end it and take the consequences. What's the worst that could happen, I asked her, lose her job? She would work again, I told her. She couldn't stand the power he held over her any more. So, she evidently decided to end it. One morning, she came to work with a battered face. She came into my office, shut the door and cried. She had told him it was over. He told her it was over when he said so and tossed her across the room into a glass coffee table."

There was only silence from the young man, who watched and listened intently.

"A few nights later she swallowed a whole bottle of OxyContin and died."

Richard's brow grew tighter and he bowed his head with a barely perceptible nod. His eyes blinked once, the wheels were turning.

"That day in the library, I was just taking a walk," continued Remmick. "I was depressed and pissed and sad for Hilde. I was sitting at a computer in the library when I spotted him at the stacks."

Richard looked up at him again.

"I wasn't looking for him, man, I swear to god. I just wanted to be alone for a while when suddenly he appeared, invading the universe again, reading a fucking magazine like it was just another Tuesday. From that moment, until the moment I found myself surrounded by cops and security, I was taken over by something out of my control. It happened, then it stopped."

"Rage," said Richard flatly.

"What?"

"The part you said about being taken over."

Remmick almost smiled. "Alright."

"It's what your shrink said in his affidavit," said Richard. "Like temporary insanity."

Remmick was suddenly baffled. "Who the fuck are you, really?"

"It's what some of those women feel just before they finally kill the man who's been abusing them for years and years," said Richard. "They get, as you said, taken over. They act out of rage, kill him, then put down the weapon and calmly call the cops and take their chances with a jury."

"Man, you do watch a lot of television," said Remmick.

"Except you did it for her. Hilde was her name? You did it."

Remmick scratched his head and rubbed his eyes and took what he figured was a final look at Richard Morone.

Richard stood slowly and said, "I've been alone for a very long time." He looked at Remmick, eyeing him up and down for a second.

He turned and took a step towards the door, stopping, without turning around, to say one more thing.

"I got your back."

He walked deliberately to the hard metal door where a CO opened it for him, and walked out.

###

Part Two

Chapter 12

Peace had blanketed the troubled soul and offered comfort and quiet. It was home and it was warm, a soft hum of random noises hushed by dulled senses.

It started in a dark gray room that slowly lightened. There was no white beam of light. With it came a dull ache.

A while later--who knew how long -- distinct sounds, maybe someone talking, a generator off in the distance. As the sounds became more evident, the dull ache became more insistent.

Now, a smell, maybe the kitchen, Maggie cleaning like a maniac again! The scent of cleaning fluids was unmistakable-- bleach or ammonia, Clorox Clean-Up or Windex. Back home again.

Then, not.

He was jolted by a sharp, invading pain somewhere, and a sudden, bright light and voices in his right ear. His eyes moved under his lids as he struggled to open them, desperate to wake up. He could feel his breathing become more urgent, each inhalation injecting pain, the noise around him becoming louder.

His eyes finally popped open and immediately closed in a pained squint. He saw a momentary silhouette of a face outlined by a blinding back-light before his eyes snapped shut again. The pain was now urgent and made him wince.

"Can you hear me?" was the question from perhaps inches in front of him. "Mr. Remmick, can you hear me?"

It was a female voice, but not his wife. Hm. Ex-wife, soon.

He reattempted opening his eyes, this time more cautiously. He identified the smell as medicinal, not kitchen. He was able to make out two people in a bright room with a white ceiling. The voice belonged to a female in an aqua outfit. He could also make out a male standing next to her. They were both looking at him as the female spoke.

"Mr, Remmick?" she asked again. "Helloooo?"

His eyes were starting to become accustomed to the light in the room which, it turned out, wasn't very bright at all. He licked his lips slowly and moved his tongue around inside his mouth.

"What?" he managed through vocal chords coated with glop. He moved his head back and forth ever so slightly to try to see more.

"Don't move around too much," said the male in the room.

Remmick closed his eyes again and took a very deep breath.

"Ow!" he yelled involuntarily.

"Don't breathe in too hard," said the same male voice.

The pain lingered for an eternity as he now identified its source-- his right side.

"What the fu--." He was unable to finish the word as another wave of pain interrupted his breathing again. "Shit god damn it!"

The male said something to the female that Remmick could not make out through his agony.

"What is going on?" he pleaded. "Where the hell--"

"You're in the hospital, Mr. Remmick," said the male. "Hunterdon Medical Center."

Remmick stared at him.

"I'm Doctor Rawandawah. You are at Hunterdon Medical Center. Do you remember what happened to you?"

Do I remember what happened, he asked himself. "I'm sorry" were the last words he remembered. Levon said them.

Remmick tried to move his hand to the source of his pain, but the doctor stopped him. "Don't try to touch it. You'll disturb the stitches."

"Sorry for what?" Remmick asked Levon.

In another moment, he felt something hard dig into his side, way in, taking his breath away, hurting him. Bad.

"Stitches?" said Remmick. "What for?"

"To close the very deep stab wound that collapsed your lung," replied the doctor.

Remmick's vision suddenly cleared and his hearing was sharp again and he smelled traces of, maybe, Old Spice.

"Oh, shit," he said as he exhaled carefully.

He couldn't shout or cry out. He couldn't breathe as his knees collapsed under him. He found himself on all fours on the cold floor of the cell, blood dripping from somewhere.

"I really am sorry." Levon sounded like he meant it.

The female reappeared at his bedside with a syringe. She flashed a smile.

"I'm Tara, your nurse," she said. "This is a little morphine."

"No shit," Remmick said. "Morphine?"

The young woman injected the clear solution into his IV. He felt nothing as she did so.

"Don't get too used to it," the doctor said with a slight grin. "It's only for the first day or so."

It reminded him of his last moments of consciousness as the shank went into his side, as his knees hit the cell floor, as he passed out and thought he would die.

He felt lightheaded now, just as he did then. Except this time, it was good.

The next time he woke up, it was less painful, less disorienting. He surfaced from a nice sleep and remembered right away where he was. There was no dull ache.

He blinked his eyes open all the way and pivoted his head first to the left, then to the right, scanning the room. Standing where the doctor and nurse had stood the last time was another male, familiar, though the name escaped him, eyeing him up as he lay there.

Remmick attempted to focus.

"Hey," said the male figure whose hands were in his pockets, a dark suit jacket over matching pants.

"You," answered Remmick, now recognizing the prison superintendent.

"Yeah," said the super. "We meet again."

Remmick closed his eyes tightly, then reopened them. He was still there. "What?"

"Just checking up on you," said the superintendent.

"Why?" asked Remmick dryly.

The superintendent's demeanor was different, more relaxed. His face looked less hard. Maybe it was the suit.

"Well, you made quite a first impression," replied the superintendent in a quiet voice. "I was wondering if you'd survive."

Remmick was annoyed that his jailer would come to his hospital bed and engage in sarcasm-- or was it his idea of irony? Remmick didn't have the energy to formulate a pithy comeback.

"Do you remember what happened?" said the super.

Remmick stared at the ceiling for a moment before saying, "I think Levon stabbed me."

"You are correct," confirmed the super. "And he has been dealt with."

"I didn't do shit to him," added Remmick. "We came back from dinner. We were moving around in the cell and a minute later, he's telling me he's sorry."

"Yea, he told me he was sorry, too."

Remmick flashed an incredulous look. "And then, I'm on the floor, bleeding. I woke up here."

"Yep." The superintendent shuffled a couple steps closer to Remmick's bed, keeping his hands in his pockets. "He used a shank made from a Bic pen and a shard of metal bent into a blade about a half-inch wide. Probably got it from inside that laptop you were using."

"What?"

"You had a laptop for a while there."

"It never left my sight."

"Evidently, it did. He knew what to remove to keep it looking intact. The COs who inspected it each evening never noticed anything missing."

Remmick was left breathless again. He was looking far beyond the super by now. "But I didn't do anything to him. I thought we were friends."

"Yea. That's why he's sorry."

Remmick picked up on something. "Well, at least there's that," he said, looking away, disgusted. "Fucker."

"His brothers basically told him to do it. They didn't like your friendship, if that's what it was."

Remmick looked at him in disbelief, then cracked a tortured grin. "So, like in 7th grade, he had to prove he liked them better than me?"

"Exactly."

"And now?"

"Oh, he proved himself-- attempted murder, assault with a deadly weapon, transferred to Montville State, maximum security, administrative segregation, etcetera, etcetera. Good for him, I say. Another victory for the bottom feeders. Yay, prison gangs."

Remmick started to formulate a response, then thought better of it and just lay there quietly.

"If it's any consolation," continued the super, "there's very little chance he will ever get out of prison. You, on the other hand, will be out in less than two."

The super turned and started walking towards the door, never removing his hands from his pockets. "You got a gift with that sentence. And now, another gift-- you're not dead."

"Um," Remmick managed. "What's your name?"

The superintendent turned to face him. "John Unger."

"Warden Unger," repeated Remmick.

"Well, Superintendent Unger, technically. But you can call me John."

Remmick just stared at him.

John Unger turned again and continued walking out, leaving Remmick staring.

###

Good evening. The man who pleaded guilty to the bizarre bookshelf killing of Kaleidoscope chief Ronald Morone two years ago has become the victim of a prison attack himself. State police say Bordon Remmick, who admitted pushing bookshelves onto Morone in the Kaleidoscope library in 2004, was stabbed by another inmate inside his cell at Kings Pointe Prison. Remmick is in critical but stable condition at Hunterdon Medical Center recovering from a collapsed lung. Prison officials say the alleged assailant, Levon Samuels, crafted a shank out of a pen and a piece of metal taken out of a laptop computer. Samuels, who had been doing time for manslaughter in the death of his wife, is now charged with attempted murder and has been transferred to Montville State Prison.

Maggie Remmick never watched the news on television anymore. Enough was enough after Bud's library escapade. But she was an incurable computer geek, logging on five, six times a day to check email and Facebook. She usually ignored the news on her Yahoo home page until the afternoon her soon-to-be ex-husband's face appeared there.

She was not allowed to visit him at the hospital. She called first and got the HIPAA lecture, then got into her car and drove to the hospital only to be turned away at the information desk. As she settled back into the drivers' seat of the Subaru, she looked out over the asphalt parking lot asking herself why her first impulse was to go to him. She couldn't find the answer, so she dug out her cell phone and dialed Arnie Shapiro.

Arnie, on the other hand, lived his life in front of the television and found out what happened to Bud Remmick while watching CNN. It stole his attention away from a case file for a minute or two, leaving him shaking his head before he went back to reading legal briefs.

His phone rang.

"Yes?"

"Mrs. Remmick on line one."

"OK."

He punched the blinking button. "Maggie. I just heard."

"I can't talk to him or see him," she said. "They won't let me."

"I gotta tell you, Mags, I'm not sure that's a good idea anyway."

"Yea," she said. "I know."

"I understand that it might be your first instinct," he offered.

It irritated her that Arnie could read her like that.

"But given the circumstances--"

"Yes, I get it, Arnie," she spat back. "I just-- fuck, I don't know."

"What would you like me to do?" he asked in a neutral voice.

She contemplated for a few seconds. "Nothing."

"I think that's probably best any--"

Click, then dial tone.

###

By the third day, Remmick was being forced to sit up in bed, stand on the floor and take a few steps around the room. He recalled the words of Jim Brady, Ronald Reagan's press secretary, who spoke of his post-shooting experience in rehab and his "physical terrorist". How perfect.

Breathing-in had gotten much easier. Now, he feared only sneezing. He thought of Maggie. It would have been nice to see her.

His physical terrorist took him for a nice walk up and down the hallway. A CO in a suit and tie was never far behind. The aluminum walker made Remmick feel like a little old man.

He returned to his room, exhausted and achy. He slowly climbed into bed and maneuvered his torso gently as he slid his butt up and onto the center of the hospital mattress. It hung out of the hospital gown, but what the hell. He was settling in to watch television, fumbling with the remote, when the superintendent appeared at the door.

Remmick was both irritated and, grudgingly, uplifted at having a visitor, though he would have preferred another individual.

"Hello," said Superintendent Unger.

"Hello," replied Remmick with a small nod. "You're here again."

"Don't sound so thrilled," said Unger.

Remmick continued moving deliberately in the bed, attempting to find a position that might be comfortable for more than a couple minutes. His attention was focused on the clunky remote control.

"You'll be going back tomorrow," Unger said without emotion. "The prison doc will keep an eye on you."

"Got another swell roommate lined up for me?"

Unger looked down at one of his shoes, then back up at Remmick. "No, you'll be in a single cell for the foreseeable future."

Remmick was playing with the channel selector and turning the volume up.

"Your wife wants to see you," Unger said.

Remmick continued messing with the remote as he answered, "Ex-wife. Soon to be."

Unger's brow tightened a bit. "Oh. I'm sorry to hear that."

Remmick turned quickly to Unger. "What does she want?"

"I don't know," replied Unger. "But you can see her for fifteen minutes if you want, tomorrow back at King's Pointe, when you see the doc. I can cut you some--"

"Forget it," Remmick said quickly, almost shouting. "I don't need—I don't— this piece of shit."

He got frustrated with the remote because the buttons were worn and sluggish.

"Ah, fuck it," he spat, tossing the device overboard to dangle by the wire connecting it to the wall. He dropped his head backwards onto his pillow and stared straight up.

"So," Unger began again, "you don't remember me, do you?"

Remmick closed his eyes and took pleasure in being able to take a breath without pain. "Yes, your office. And you were here the other day."

"No, I mean--"

Unger stopped, contemplating his next words. "Yea, that's right, checking up on you."

"It was a touching gesture, really," said Remmick with as much sarcasm as he could muster.

Unger stared at the wounded man in the hospital bed. Remmick could feel it.

"Anything else?" he asked, his eyes still closed.

"No," replied Unger. "See you back at the ranch."

Remmick inhaled another breath of recycled hospital air and opened his eyes to look at the Superintendent, but he was gone.

###

Chapter 13

Bordon Remmick returned to being number 5816774 the next day, as promised. He was led off the small, white bus and through the double gates in handcuffs. The very specific smell of the sweaty, vinyl seats inside of the bus brought back the sensations of his first day at Kings Pointe-- ambivalence, fear and wonder, all mixed together and cooking in the pit of his stomach. His stay at the hospital made him feel almost normal, except for the wound on his right side, of course. Coming back to prison was like starting over again. Only this time, he was one of them and had been for two years.

He briefly remembered the scene in The Shawshank Redemption in which the new arrivals are filed past a gauntlet of hooting and hissing inmates, eyeing them up and shouting nastiness and threats. There was no such reception for Remmick. His bus was met by two CO's who accompanied him across the 20-foot walkway to the heavy steel door that led to the next two years of his life.

Within ten minutes of his return, inmate Remmick had been stripped down, searched head to toe, wrapped in another open-backed gown and seated on an examination table in the prison infirmary. Unlike Hunterdon Medical Center, the prison infirmary was chilly and echoed with voices ricocheting off the high ceiling and stainless steel fixtures. Missing were the tightly dressed and coifed nurses who padded silently on a waxed floor. There was a doctor, one indifferent nurse and two trustees who did paperwork and cleaning, and Bud Remmick sitting on the edge of a metal table.

After a wait of about two minutes, a man dressed in khaki pants and an open-collared white shirt came over to him.

"I'm Doctor Colima," he said, without looking Remmick in the eye. "Let's see that." He began removing the bandage on Remmick's right side. He worked quickly and without a hint of dexterity, jamming blunt-ended scissors between the folds of gauze and under the tape, yanking, twisting and cutting. Miraculously, he didn't actually cut skin. After what seemed to Remmick an eternity, several chunks of bandage were removed, enough to expose the short line of stitches and the purple swatches of skin they held together. Remmick saw the actual wound for the first time-- only 3 or 4 stitches over a very small laceration.

"Christ, that's it?" he said as he stared at his side. "That little thing?"

"You were expecting a Spielberg movie?" responded the doctor, again without looking up at Remmick. He touched it with a gloved finger, poking it slightly. "Bet that hurt like a mother fucker."

"Yes, and I'm not loving the poking," snapped Remmick.

Colima took his finger away and reached for a large x-ray sitting on another table a few feet away. He held it up to the bright, fluorescent fixture overhead.

"Deep wound," he said to the x-ray. "See?" He pointed to a thin line that cut into what appeared to be Remmick's side and lung.

Remmick squinted to see and followed the doctor's finger. It was the path the shiv took as it punctured his pleural cavity and right lung. It went on forever.

Colima put the x-ray back on the table and picked up a bottle of red solution, some cotton balls and a handful of fresh bandages. Without speaking, and without looking at Remmick, he grabbed a few cotton balls with tongs and soaked them in the red liquid, then swabbed Remmick's stitched wound. In the few seconds it took to dry, the doctor had torn open two five-by-nine gauze pads and a roll of two-inch tape. He slapped the five-by-nines up against the wound with one hand and used the fingers of the same hand to undo the tape from the roll, which he held in the other hand. Remmick was amused and annoyed as the doctor ripped large strips of tape from the roll in this awkward position and somehow managed to get two to stick to the gauze and his skin at the same time. With both hands free, Colima started unrolling tape like he was packing a FedEx box, slapping it onto Remmick's side. Several minutes later, the gauze pads were completely covered in white tape. The doctor put down the tape roll and looked satisfied as he eyeballed the wound one last time.

"You can get dressed," he said and walked into an office and closed the door. He was replaced in another moment by a CO who handed Remmick his boxers, sweat pants, shirt and sandals and stood there while Remmick put them on. He moved carefully, still guarding his right side. Once he was dressed, the CO made a motion towards the heavy door that led to the hallway that would lead to Remmick's new cell.

"Great to be back," mumbled Remmick as he trudged slowly past the CO.

###

One hour and 19-minutes later, Remmick was sitting in the visitor's room, possibly at the same metal table where they last met, averting the eyes of Margaret Remmick.

"What's the point?" he asked, suddenly looking into her eyes.

She waited for more. There was only his icy stare. This was someone other than the man she married. She turned her head down.

"For some reason," she began, still looking down, "when I heard about the stabbing, my first instinct was to go to you."

He continued looking at her, hoping she would raise her eyes to his again.

"Arnie advised against it," she continued.

"Arnie?"

She nodded a little. "Well, he is my lawyer."

"Yes," he responded. "Arnie's your lawyer." He waited for more from her, then asked, "What else is Arnie?"

Her head snapped up and her eyes locked onto his. "Nothing," she spat.

He was surprised by her reaction.

"Not one, fucking thing," she said, her voice raising in volume a notch.

"Ok, ok," he responded, holding his hands up.

Her eyes stayed on his for another moment, then dropped again as she said, "I threatened to cut off his hand with my Swiss Army knife."

Remmick's gaze immediately softened and traces of a smile formed at the corners of his mouth. She continued looking down, but gave a grin. "I think that cured him."

Remmick extended his hand onto the table and she immediately took it. Their eyes met and they smiled weakly at each other. The CO in the corner cleared his throat so they could hear, a cue that they shouldn't be touching.

"I thought about you in the hospital," he admitted. "I wished you were there."

"I tried, but they wouldn't let me in."

"Oh. You came?"

"Yea, I came," she said. "I told you, it was my first instinct."

"I'm sorry," he said, but didn't elaborate.

She searched his eyes for the meaning of those two words.

"I'm sorry," he repeated, grasping her hand more tightly.

Her eyes locked on his. She felt emotion welling up and fought it.

The CO took a step towards them. Remmick immediately picked up on it and let go of Maggie's hand. The CO immediately stopped and returned to his post.

"The warden, er, superintendent," Remmick said, "wants to be my new best friend. He visited me twice in the hospital."

Maggie nodded in acknowledgement. "Yea, he's the only reason they let me see you this soon. He was really nice to me on the phone."

"I don't understand it," said Remmick, "especially after what I did to his office."

"What did you do to his office?" she asked with a bit of alarm in her voice.

"I had a moment," he replied. "Let's just leave it at that."

She nodded and, reluctantly, let it go. "Well, maybe he feels he still owes you."

Remmick's face went blank. "Huh?"

"You know, for the Graterford thing."

He continued to stare at her like she was insane, squinting his eyes and shaking his head, completely clueless.

"Oh my god," she said, finally getting it. "You don't remember him, do you?"

Remmick now stared beyond her, his mind searching memories with the keyword GRATERFORD. There was the riot that one night at Graterford Prison outside of Philly in the late 80's.

"The prison riot?" he asked out loud.

"Yea," she replied, nodding.

He continued staring past her, but now he started remembering. After working his full shift on the assignment desk one night, a riot broke out in the prison. He grabbed a photographer and his only remaining resource at 12:30am-- Maggie the Intern-- and went to the prison to cover until a reporter and live truck could get there. The drive through Montgomery County was bleak in the dark and the rain, but they made it in less than 45 minutes. At the main gate, Remmick and his photog showed their press cards. They had to talk Maggie in. They were directed to the visitors' parking lot, parked the van, unloaded the camera and trotted into the only door they could find. The unmarked door had a heavy glass window. They pulled it open and were greeted by two men, heavily armed.

"Over there," one of them said, pointing to another door in an alcove.

The trio walked to that door and opened it, walking into the main visitor's area, a room with metal tables and a number of heavy, wooden chairs. One of the tables had a piece of 8-1/2" x 11" paper laying on it with the word PRESS scrawled onto it in black marker. No one else was there yet.

The photographer found a table he liked and put his gear on it. Maggie sat in a chair next to his. Remmick looked around the room.

"I gotta go to the bathroom," he announced. Another armed guard pointed him through another door.

"About 15 feet down that hall, then a right," he said.

Remmick walked through the door which led into a short hallway. He walked about 10 feet down the hall before he heard sounds and a voice coming from somewhere. Five more feet and the sound was louder. He was soon in front of a door on the right side of the hallway that had a sign with the word MEN in white letters over a black rectangle. He heard a sound come from inside he couldn't make out.

Remmick opened the door and hoped the urinal would be right there. Instead, his arrival froze a violent scene-- a man in a uniform had just landed a booted kick against the head of another man who was on the floor, face down, hands cuffed behind his back. The man on the floor didn't move. Blood flowed from his nose. The uniformed man's foot was now parked on the neck and he locked his eyes onto Remmick's. Sweat dripped from the tip of the man's nose, onto the body beneath his foot. Remmick followed the path of the sweat drop from the foot, back up to its source. His eyes stopped at a small pin attached to the guard's white collar. It was gold in the shape of a tiny magic wand with a gold starburst attached to the end.

Remmick's head suddenly unfroze and his eyes clicked back to their original purpose-- scanning the room to find a place to piss. As his eyes scanned, the uniformed man's eyes followed his. Remmick made his way quickly and quietly to the urinal, his pants unzipped and penis halfway out well before he got there. The relief was instantaneous and overwhelming. He stood there for what seemed an eternity, not daring to even glance over his shoulder. Finally, he zipped up and turned to the same scene that greeted him as he walked in.

The guard stared down at the inmate he'd been kicking. The inmate was still breathing. Remmick quickly looked at his own face in the mirror, turned once more to look at the guard, who kept his head down now. No words were spoken. Then, Remmick turned to the door and left the bathroom, walking quickly and quietly the way he came, back to the visitor's room.

By 4:15am, the riot had been quelled. The sleepy reporters and photographers were roused by the prison superintendent, a man named Larchmont or Larchwood, who came into the visitor's room to a spot where a rickety podium had been wheeled in, accompanied by an entourage of sullen but relieved looking men. He announced that the riot had been contained, all the inmates were back in their cells, a lockdown was underway and a cache of weapons, including a dozen or so crude knives and one shotgun taken from a murdered guard, had been recovered.

"The ringleaders have been identified," continued Larchmont. "John, please tell them about that part of it."

Larchmont ceded the podium to a uniformed man who had been behind him and who was now stepping to the podium. Remmick's eyes nearly popped out of his head as they were drawn instantly to the gold pin on the uniformed man's shirt collar. As the man stepped to the podium and looked at the group of reporters, his eyes met Remmick's, an icy stare that froze them both to their spots on the floor. At that moment, no one else was in the room. And then, the man named John broke the stare and began speaking.

"Our investigation discovered a plot that had been in the making for several months," he began. The story went on for a few minutes. The room was quiet as the reporters allowed the man to tell the story. Then, he stopped talking. He stepped back to his original spot and was replaced by the superintendent.

"We'll take a few questions," he said.

Remmick immediately cried out. "Um, about the plot..."

Larchmont turned to the man named John and motioned him to take the podium again. Remmick resumed. "Was it, um, another inmate who told you about it?"

"Our investigation involved information developed at several levels," the man replied with no emotion. "That's all I can say."

It wasn't until the next day that Remmick told Maggie what he had seen in the bathroom. He never told anyone else. He'd learned the man was a highly regarded, career corrections officer, whose information was credited with breaking the inmates' communications network and recovering the missing shotgun.

"Christ," Remmick breathed to his almost-ex. "The name didn't compute. Didn't he have--"

"More hair," Maggie said. "Yea."

Remmick and Maggie looked into each other's eyes for a moment, recapturing the event from their past.

"You could have ratted him out that day," Maggie reminded him.

Remmick's gaze betrayed that he had gone somewhere else -- back to that day in Unger's office, moments after he destroyed the glass case, moments after the guards came rushing in with rifles pointed at him, as the superintendent spoke, strangely calm.

"...you think about not only what you did here, but what really made you do it. Anger like yours will destroy you. I know this."

Maggie caught her almost-ex-husband nodding a little.

"Yes?" she queried.

His head was stuck in the downward motion of a nod, sinking to the level of his rounded shoulders. His lips were parted slightly. His breathing was steady and quicker than usual. His hands lay limp on his thighs. His eyes fixed on a scratch on the metal table top.

He couldn't muster the energy to take a deep breath, so he spoke on a weak exhale.

"Fuck me."

The words barely escaped his lips.

"What is it?" asked Maggie in a voice equally weak.

Remmick felt something in the pit of his stomach, an emotion he had been trying for the longest time not to feel.

"I don't know how to--," he said with a quiver in his voice.

Maggie knew.

All his trouble, all his anger.

"I don't fucking know," he answered an unasked question.

Maggie looked into him. She knew the other man who lived inside him.

"Bud?" she asked mildly.

He looked up at her, tears welling from the pools in his eyes onto his face, flowing down slowly as his lower lip quivered like a first grader on the first day of school.

"I'm so--"

The CO who had been watching them moved towards them and said, "Time's up."

Remmick looked up at the guard, and back at Maggie, then slowly slid his chair back and stood up. He wiped his face with his hands, sniffling and breathing through his mouth.

Maggie's eyes never left his as the guard approached, placed Remmick's hands behind him and cuffed them. As he was led out of the room, Remmick sniffed loudly and shuffled slowly back to his cell.

###

Chapter 14

The ratty bench had been repaired more than once and the paint job was now a toxic collection of shards aimed at the buttocks and thighs of anyone contemplating sitting down. It was an act of conscious self-injury to sit there. Yet, Richard Morone found a spot, cleared by hand of the worst of the peeling paint. As he had so many times during his life, he weighed the potential for pain against the need of the moment, always willing to compromise, never accepting the completely pain-free option.

He sat with his knees together, feet flat on the ground and his hands folded on his lap, as though awaiting a lesson. The jogging path was about 20-feet behind the bench and he heard the occasional runner clip by. He looked straight ahead at the tiny pond, its still water green with mysterious sub-surface growth and occasional flicks on the water's glassy top. The air was still and it smelled of soil and damp moss.

He tilted his head slightly downward towards the young woman who sat on the ground by his feet. She also stared out at the pond. Her brown hair, unbrushed and a bit scattered, extended well below her shoulders. Morone studied the part on top of her head. It was directly in the middle, and straight. As he stared at her, she slowly turned her head towards him, catching his gaze with one eye. His eye focused on her lovely green iris, not at the bright red blotch in her sclera and not on the angry, purple, golf-ball sized welt on her right cheek. They stared at each other for a few seconds, he completely immobile, she gently running her tongue over her swollen, black, lacerated upper lip. As her tongue touched the gash, she flinched slightly, then retracted her tongue. Their eyes remained locked and she offered an ever-so-subtle smile.

Morone turned his gaze back out to the pond, a sight which offered no complexity. Without moving his head, he reached into his back pocket and withdrew his wallet. He looked down and dug in to find three, 100-dollar bills. He withdrew them and held them out. The young woman looked at the money and took it. She slowly eased herself up onto her feet, stuffed the money into a pocket in her jeans and walked away without saying a word.

Richard Morone remained on the bench, staring first at his bandaged right hand, then back out at the pond.

###

Chapter 15

Arnie Shapiro always knew a good potential client when he saw one. Back when he found Bud Remmick at that bar, he knew the drunk was in trouble. Several years later, when he figured Lee Solomon's talent as an investment banker would eventually lead him to invest, then steal someone else's money, he was there to represent him. Solomon went to jail but Arnie billed $130,000.

And when Richard Morone walked into his office and introduced himself, Arnie immediately felt that old familiar tingling at the nape of his neck. Richard Morone, son of victim Ronald Morone, who was killed by client Bud Remmick. Was it a conflict of interest?

"There's no conflict," Arnie replied to Morone's question. "Remmick is convicted, jailed and no appeals are pending. He has cut me loose."

This last part was true in Arnie's mind, though Remmick might have disagreed. Arnie chose not to share that he was also representing Maggie Remmick in the divorce.

"What can I do for you, sir?" asked Arnie in his most condescending voice.

Morone had sat in the same chair Maggie Remmick had sat in just days before, moving the fingers of his bandaged hand, making a fist, then releasing it.

"I want to help him," he said, examining his hand.

"Who?" queried Arnie, incredulously. "Bud Remmick?"

Morone's eyes moved to Arnie's. His face was blank. He nodded.

"How come?" asked Arnie sharply.

Morone studied Arnie's puzzled face for a moment, then took a breath and said, while exhaling, "He did a great service."

Arnie's eyes narrowed.

"What, killing your old man?"

Morone's eyes were still locked on Arnie's. He nodded again. Arnie noticed he was lightly chewing something, maybe gum.

"Wow," Arnie offered with his weasel grin. "That's different."

Morone shrugged.

"What did you have in mind," asked Arnie.

"I was hoping you could tell me," Morone replied.

"His first bid for parole was denied, you know," offered Arnie. "Jailhouse misbehavior."

"I met with him recently," said Morone. "I visited him."

"Really? Why?"

"I wanted him to know I'd been following the case," Morone said. "I wasn't sure what to expect when I met him. But after we talked, I think we came to an understanding."

"Oh, yea?" said Arnie, a bit wide-eyed. "About what?"

"Something we have in common," Morone answered cryptically. "I'll leave it at that."

Arnie, who had been standing a couple feet from where Morone was sitting, turned and went to his desk, sitting down deliberately.

"His next parole hearing is next month," he said. "Parole boards are often moved by victim statements, statements from family members, gestures of forgiveness--"

"So, letters?"

"Letters are OK, but in-person testimony is best," said Arnie. "At the next parole hearing, showing up and doing a pitch for him might have significant impact."

"Enough to grant him parole?"

"Maybe."

Arnie became uncharacteristically thoughtful. "I don't really know."

Morone sat quietly nodding, his eyes staring off.

"It's a shame," resumed Arnie, "that I don't really give a shit about Bud Remmick anymore. Otherwise, I might be more helpful."

Morone's gaze re-focused on Arnie. "Would money increase the Give-A-Shit Factor?"

Arnie held Morone's stare. His answer came without emotion. "Yes."

Morone's eyes never left Arnie's. "What if I hired you as my attorney with the sole mission of helping to get Bud Remmick released on parole?"

Arnie could usually pick up on a nuanced scam. Not this time. He looked sideways at Morone, literally.

"OK, man, I don't fucking get it," he said with a little petulance. "You're gonna pay me to help you get Bud Remmick out on parole?"

"Yes," Morone answered, simply.

"And all because he did this great service by knocking off your old man?"

Morone simply looked straight at him.

"He's only got two years to go on the gift of a sentence I got for him," said Arnie, bitterly. "What's the hurry?"

"Mr. Shapiro," began Morone.

"Please, Arnie,"

"Mr. Shapiro, my reasons would probably only confuse you," said Morone. "You don't actually care, as you just said, what happens to Mr. Remmick. So, let's not waste our time by me trying to explain it to you."

Arnie looked, not insulted, but relieved, then said, "Twenty-five thousand."

Morone didn't blink, but nodded almost imperceptibly.

"Half today," Arnie added quickly.

Morone had no reaction other than to say, "OK."

"OK," answered Arnie, who extended his hand. Morone first inspected Arnie's hand, then took it and shook once.

Morone broke his eyes away from Arnie's, took his hand back and in two quick steps left Arnie's office, closing the door behind him.

Arnie looked at the closed door for a moment, then spun around and headed to his desk. He sat down and immediately picked up the phone and dialed a number.

Maggie Remmick sat on the front porch of the home she once shared with her husband, staring at her iPad, flicking through pages of news stories, scanning local real estate sites, dropping in on Ebay, checking her unread email. She could only do that for so long before her mind went back to Bud.

She wanted to believe that what she was feeling was only an annoying twinge of guilt. Yet, it was persistent and daily. It was a question.

Do you still love him?

A loud motorcycle zipped by the house. She tried to get a good look at who was driving. It was the asshole who lived up the street. She realized he was only an asshole because he disturbed her at that moment. She couldn't swear that he was, in reality, an asshole.

Do you still love him?

It wasn't a voice that asked the question, but more like an electronic read-out of text that flashed in her brain.

She couldn't answer. Really, she was afraid to answer.

At last, she folded her iPad back into its case, rose from the porch chair and made her way back into the house. As she walked into the kitchen, she spied the blinking number "1" on her phone, indicating a missed message. She hadn't heard the phone ring. She pushed the PLAY button.

"Hi, Maggie. Arnie Shapiro. Call me. Something unusual has come up."

Hm.

Do you still love him?

###

Chapter 16

Remmick had not felt a twinge of remorse for Levon Samuel's fate at the hands of the prison system. After all, he did stab him with a shiv, a fate usually reserved for squealers, child molesters and homeboys gone wrong, then topped it off with an I'm sorry. Remmick supposed Levon was having a tough conversation at that moment with his Higher Power, as he did after being jailed for running over his wife in the Wendy's parking lot. Fuck Levon.

But at this moment, sitting at the hard, metal cafeteria table, twiddling his spaghetti on his fork alone, Remmick actually thought fondly of mealtimes with his former cell mate. While Remmick wasn't the world's greatest conversationalist, he did enjoy company at meal time. Ironic, that he felt even vague nostalgia for the guy who almost killed him. They shared many things during those meals. Remmick wondered what that conversation might have sounded like.

"Will you stab me in the back, chest, neck or torso?" Remmick would ask.

"Um, get you from the back, for sure."

"Yea, my choice, too, if trying to avoid confrontation."

"Oh, I don't care about confrontation," Levon would say. "I just would like to avoid an argument."

"But for absolute certainty, wouldn't it be better to choose the neck?

"Yea, but then you gotta cut the throat," Levon would muse. "Because the carotid and jugular lay just so and you'd have to aim pretty good. So, the tried and true lateral cut, ear to ear, would then be the correct choice."

"Right on."

As if on cue, Remmick winced in pain as he twisted to his right to see what all the noise was. Two tables away, several guards had converged on an inmate. Two had slammed his head onto the metal table while two others grabbed at a metallic object he held in one hand.

"Let go now!" bellowed one of the guards. The inmate twisted under the pile of uniformed men and let out a squeal before dropping the object. Remmick couldn't make out what it was. It didn't matter. In another 20 seconds, the inmate was on the floor, face down, handcuffed and shackled at the feet. Remmick spied the guards on the tier above, training their rifles out into the sea of inmates, ready to pick off any who tried to interfere.

One of the guards picked up the object, stuffed it into a pocket, then proceeded to assist in lifting the inmate off the floor to be dragged way. The dumbass certainly bought himself a month or so in A-SEG.

Remmick, nonplussed, refocused on consuming spaghetti, meatloaf and peas. So did everyone around him. Some chuckles rose up from the din of men eating.

Back in his cell, Remmick lay on his bunk, grateful for having a single, but lonely. He felt stupid for being lonely. He didn't miss Levon. He missed Maggie.

He was starting to get it. But by the time he would totally get it, would it be too late? Would she be totally over him? Would the door be permanently closed? It occurred to him that when he got out of prison, when he actually walked out the gate and stood there in the parking lot with his small bag of possessions and $100 in cash, he might have to find a taxi. Or a bus.

This is what he thought about, supine on his bunk, well into his third year of incarceration.

###

Chapter 17

Superintendent Unger sat at his desk, thumbing through inmate files, one after another. They were new arrivals. He looked for anomalies, dysfunction, signs of mental illness, behavioral history, reports of self-injury and other red flags. Kings Pointe was supposed to be for inmates who weren't yet hard core. But recent events, not the least of which included the assault on Borden Remmick, a fire set by another inmate and the cafeteria event, made him look more closely for signs of impending trouble.

Unger had been in on the ground floor of the design of Kings Pointe. A veteran of Graterford in Pennsylvania and a brief stint on Riker's Island after that, Unger had seen the worst the prison system had to offer. He had hoped that Kings Pointe would be a model of modern design—clean, humane, multiple sources of natural light, more ergonomically designed living spaces, brighter paint—stronger cell walls and locks. When men are treated like men, he reasoned, the prison environment could be tolerable for all concerned. Gone were the days of violent confrontations in which guards had to assert control at every turn, mercilessly and coldly, lest the inmate with ideas of control were to get a foothold. It was a fine concept, five years ago.

Unger's concept soon began to sag under the weight of the burgeoning inmate population. The tidy plan to segregate medium security prisoners from the baddest actors became a subject of wistful conversation in the CO's break room. Prison space was shrinking in a country which locks up more people than any other. And New Jersey had more than its share of felons who were either violent when they arrived, or became violent after a while behind bars. The system wasn't totally lost, but it was getting there.

His intercom buzzed to life.

"Margaret Remmick is on the line."

"Thanks," said Unger, pausing for a moment before picking up the phone and punching the blinking button. He snapped up the receiver.

"Hello?"

"Hello, Mr. Unger," came Maggie's voice.

"Hi. Please call me John."

"Hi," she said again.

"What can I do for you?"

He heard her take a breath and pause.

"Well," she began, "I was wondering if you could help me with something."

###

Chapter 18

"I was only eight years old but I could fix a flat tire on my bike just fine. Flat tires were common since the driveway had all kinds of hazards lurking--sharp pieces of concrete, roofing nails, god knows what else. I always kept a kit handy, a Tire Repair Kit I got for a couple bucks at the Penn Jersey Auto Supply store on Rising Sun Avenue. It came in a can that contained a couple rubber patches and a small tube of rubber cement. The operation would always take place outside my back door, half in the common driveway. I would turn the bike upside down, resting it on its seat and handle bars, then use a wrench to remove the wheel with the flat tire. The rear wheel was more complicated because you had to unthread the chain and watch out for the greasy sprocket, but it was a no brainer. The tricky part was prying the tire off the wheel rim without puncturing the tube.

"I made this repair a dozen times and could do it with my eyes closed. One day, mostly likely out of utter boredom, I attracted a small crowd of friends from the neighborhood--Chucky, my best friend, Johnny from across the driveway and the other Johnny from up the street, plus Johnny-from-across-the-driveway's brother Mikey and I think maybe Nancy who lived on the corner. We all shared this driveway that ran the length of our row homes' back entrances, so wandering from house to house was no big deal.

"On that one particular day, when it came time to get the tire off the rim, the only tool I could find was a chisel. In the past, I'd used a wide-bladed screwdriver, but there wasn't one to be found. So, I found a chisel on a shelf in the basement, which had an even wider blade that I thought would actually work better than a screwdriver. My friends had gathered to watch me work and my dad, who heard me rooting around in the basement, appeared as well.

"As I began prying the tire off with the chisel, my dad laid into me. 'What the hell are you doing?' he said loudly. 'You're using a chisel for this?'

"Chucky started giggling. 'Are you an idiot?' dad shrieked. 'That's the wrong tool to use for this! Since when do you use a chisel to pry off a tire?'

"All my friends were now laughing. 'Move away,' said my dad as he grabbed the chisel out of my hand and half-pushed me out of the way. 'You obviously have no idea what you're doing.'

"I was eight. I was destroyed and humiliated. Of course, I started crying, which only made everyone laugh harder. I ran into the house, up to my room and stayed there for the rest of the afternoon. I've never forgotten that day."

Father Timmons leaned back in his chair and gave Remmick a steady stare that paved the way for his next question.

"And that's why you hate authority figures?" he asked with a raised eyebrow.

"He wouldn't let me wear bell-bottoms, or wear a peace symbol when I was 16," Remmick replied. "He was never happy with a C on a report card, not one fucking C was permitted. When I had to bail out of advanced classes in high school because they were too hard, he was crushed. I got a bunch of guilt-lectures about how I wouldn't get into any good colleges if I kept getting C's."

Father Timmons shifted in his seat again, still wondering.

"And?" he queried.

"And what?" answered Remmick.

"What else? Did you beat you? Did he abuse you?"

"No," said Remmick. "Occasional spankings with an open hand, which were inconsequential."

"So then, this is why you have problems with authority figures?" Timmons was incredulous. "Everything you describe, with the possible exception of the chisel over-reaction, sounds like pretty normal stuff."

"I never felt anything I did was good enough," replied Remmick.

"That, too--"

"Jesus, really?" spat Remmick. "What do you want, blood?"

"Um, no, I don't want anything," said Timmons. "I'm just trying to understand where your anger comes from."

"What anger?"

Timmons' eyes grew wider and a barely perceptible smile appeared.

Remmick immediately lowered his eyes.

"Bud," Father Timmons finally offered. "Why on earth are you here? You can't blame your father, I don't think, for pushing those shelves onto Ronald Morone."

Remmick gestured to Father Timmons to move closer. Father leaned across the metal table so Remmick could get closer to his ear to speak quietly and evenly.

"I don't like being told what to do," said Remmick in a quiet monotone. "I don't like bullies. I don't like being mocked. I don't like seeing weak people being bullied or mocked."

The two men separated and sat back in their chairs again.

"I don't know what else to tell you," Remmick said in summary. "Somewhere in my brain, Morone pushed all those buttons--"

Timmons took a breath as though to speak and was almost knocked off his chair.

"AND NOW HE'S DEAD!" boomed Remmick.

Several sets of shocked eyes locked onto Remmick as the CO approached and Father Timmons reeled.

"And I'm not fucking sorry," Remmick added as the guard reapplied his shackles and started moving him out of the visitors' area and back to his cell.

"He's not making it any easier," Unger said into his cellphone.

"Yea," replied Maggie Remmick. "He's got a thing-- he knows it."

"What? What is the goddam thing?"

"A dysfunction. Immaturity. Paranoia? I could never really place it."

"No one knows him better than you," Unger reminded her.

"He doesn't talk about it," Maggie said. "I never made him talk about it."

"Because he never killed anyone before?"

Several seconds of silence.

"Yea, I guess so."

"Yet, he's got this capacity for, um-- I don't know--"

"Compassion. Forgiveness. Fairness. His employees have always loved him. I've always loved him."

Unger considered that for a moment. "Yet he doesn't love himself." He heard the words exit and immediately regretted it, sounding like an amateur shrink.

"He's tried very hard to, um," began Maggie, her voice quivering, then quickly melting into a muted sob. "He's tried to figure it out."

Unger took a deep breath, as if to clear the air.

"He has a little less than a year on his sentence now," he said. "Maybe this next hearing is more about him getting squared away inside and less about getting out early."

Maggie sniffed into the phone.

"Squared away, huh? Just like that."

"There can't be a next time, Mrs. Remmick," replied Unger. "He got off easily this time because he had no criminal record and a great lawyer. If he does violence of any kind again, he'll go away for a much longer time."

"Thank you for your kindness," Maggie said in a stronger, sincere voice. "He will eventually come around." She clicked off her phone.

Unger sat in the silence of his office.

"I don't know about that," he said to no one.

###

Chapter 19

Arnie Shapiro's voice rose as he scolded his newest client across his desk.

"You can't go in there and say you support Bud Remmick because he killed your prick of a father. You might as well tell them he killed Mother fucking Teresa."

Richard Morone looked at him impatiently.

"Really, Mr. Shapiro. Do you think I'm an idiot?"

"Then what is your plan?" asked Arnie.

"It'll be fine," replied Richard. "I'm working on her now." He stood up and reached across the desk to shake Arnie's hand. "Don't worry."

Arnie reluctantly shook his hand. "That's all the fuck I do, man."

###

Part 3

Chapter 20

There was no light, no dark.

A wash of silenced sensation enveloped him as he sat with his head in his hands. The edge of his cot was unforgiving against his coccyx.

There was no going back.

Bud Remmick, born to German parents who came to the US and made a decent life for him, educated and vetted by his peers, liked by many, loved by one, confronted the deal he made with himself to live with his crime without remorse, do the time and then get on with his life.

If only.

The soft simplicity he believed in almost four years ago had slowly twisted into a knot of vile reality. And with his face buried in his palms and his neck hanging crooked and feet flat on the concrete floor of his cell, Bud Remmick finally got it.

He felt the dull, nagging pain at the site of his wound, a reminder he would always carry. He saw Maggie's face floating in the air, tears flowing as she related stories of her shitty new life, an image that kept him awake at night. He was haunted by Richard Morone, whose disturbing countenance in the visitor's room and vague gleefulness over the death of his father gave Remmick a chill. The widow's blind love of a man who had abused her and her shrieking at the sentencing now had meaning. The prison superintendent's hovering at the hospital, Ray Vignola's gym wisdom and Levon's attempted murder of him, everything congealed into a softball-sized fist in Remmick's stomach, building over almost four years, nurtured by sleepless nights and an abandonment of conscience.

It was Bud Remmick's day of reckoning.

There was no speech as the CO's came to his cell to apply the handcuffs and walk him down one hallway, around to another, up a half flight of steps into a brighter wing of the prison, then a few steps down a very short hallway into a familiar room.

Seated at a table in front of the room were three people he recognized. Seated in another set of seats off to the side, almost like a jury, were people painfully familiar to him. He felt an unsettling wave of anticipation mixed with dread. He had never been in a place that panicked him like this.

He felt every set of eyeballs locked onto him as he walked into the room and towards the heavy oaken chair placed squarely before the long table. He did not return looks with anyone and in fact, after his initial glance around the room, turned his head downward as he trudged to the chair. He did not look or feel like a man who was just a few months from being released from prison. He looked every inch like a prisoner.

He felt several presences which disturbed him greatly, several which puzzled him and one which made him feel familiar and vaguely reassured, though he had trouble trusting any emotion at this point. The mix of people was confusing to him, individuals who were out of context. Was this part of a test?

He settled back into the oak chair and instantly was transported to the first meeting he'd had in this very room. Sitting at the table were the same three committee members on whom he had made such a vivid impression more than three years ago. This was not going to be good, he thought.

There were no conversations underway, no mutterings or whispers among those in the room, just rapt silence. Remmick was aware of a vague aroma of damp book pages and an even vaguer hint of cologne, a man's cologne, probably the chairman's. Today, the chairman wore a neat navy blue blazer, white shirt and a blue and black, diagonally striped tie. The red headed woman looked exactly the same, bright red hair cut short and framing a painfully white face with a burgundy shade of lip gloss. The man who reminded Remmick of George Costanza appeared to have gained weight and had even less hair than before, his beady eyes darting to the left and right behind his dark-rimmed eye glasses.

Maggie was here. Amy and Nate from Kaleidoscope were here. Karen Sikorsky from his old TV station in Philly was here, along with another former employee he had long forgotten about, photographer Keith Abramowitz. In the two end seats of the third row of chairs sat Richard Morone and, my god thought Remmick, the Widow Morone. He had forgotten her name.

In the front row sat Superintendent Ungar and Father Tim. And, Arnie Shapiro.

Remmick's eyes furtively glanced across the assembled members of his own personal Hall of Fame. He didn't feel any better than he did when he walked in.

He wished his mom and dad were here. Then again, maybe it was better that they stayed away. They kept in touch with Maggie but had no desire to visit, write or call him.

This time, the commissioners had name plates. Chairman Wilson Toohey was the first to speak.

"Good morning, ladies and gentleman," he said absently. "This is a status hearing for inmate Bordon Remmick on his four-year sentence for involuntary manslaughter."

There was still no one else speaking in the room, no noise at all, in fact. Remmick glanced quickly at Maggie. Her eyes were riveted on him. He continued to carefully move his glance to Richard Morone and his mother. They both sat staring off to a distant place, there in body only. Richard's vacant look suggested indifference. The Widow Morone's countenance made Remmick think of an old washing machine.

"There is an opportunity for early release for Mr. Remmick," continued the chairman. "Our purpose today is to see if that is warranted."

Remmick kept his head down but moved his eyes across those seated in the gallery. He had no idea what to expect.

"Superintendent Ungar, I understand you would like to make an opening statement," said Toohey.

Ungar stood up and walked towards a chair that had been set next to the committee table, a sort of witness stand. He reached into his jacket pocket and pulled out a folded piece of paper as he approached the chair and finally sat down. He unfolded the paper and adjusted its distance from his eyes. The room remained silent.

"I am John Ungar, Superintendent of Kings Pointe Correctional Institution," he began. "I support early release for Mr. Remmick. In his time here he has participated in all assigned activities according to prison regulations. He suffered a near-fatal, unprovoked attack at the hands of another inmate and has been recovering from that injury. He has expressed regret for his crime."

This made Remmick's brow furrow as he stared at Ungar, who finished reading, refolded the paper and placed it back in his pocket.

"Any questions from the panel?" queried Toohey? None were forthcoming as the redhead and George Constanza remained mute.

"Thank you, Superintendent Ungar," said Toohey as Ungar walked back to his seat in the gallery.

"The next person to speak is--"

"Excuse me, sir."

Toohey was interrupted.

"Yes, Mr. Remmick?"

"I think I can save you and all these folks here some time."

"Yes? How's that?"

Remmick shifted slightly in the oak chair. "May I speak?"

The chairman's face was the same as the last time they had met in this room--hard and uncertain at what would come out of Remmick's mouth.

"Yes, Mr. Remmick. What would you like to say?"

Remmick sat with his hands folded on his lap. He lifted his head and inhaled deeply, turning his head slightly to look at the gallery, then back again to look at the committee. He exhaled audibly.

"Um," he began tentatively. "I, ah, I need to say something now."

Toohey blinked and reset his gaze directly at Remmick's eyes. "Go ahead."

Remmick nodded almost imperceptibly.

"I appreciate you all coming here," he said to the assembled gallery. "I appreciate the superintendent's words about me. I don't know why he said them, but I appreciate it."

Ungar sat unmoving in his seat. Remmick noted that Maggie had shot a quick glance Ungar's way.

"Once, back in the newsroom, I remember watching a Pentagon news conference and heard a general answering questions about some military issue, don't remember what."

Remmick paused to see if anyone was listening. Everyone was listening.

"A reporter asked him a question he didn't know the answer to. Instead of just saying 'I don't know'"--

Remmick paused, perhaps to make sure he got the next line correct.

"He said, 'I have not achieved clarity on that issue.'"

Remmick looked up and smiled. He shot a glance at Maggie. She had a small grin. She had heard that story.

"I thought that was the most bureaucratic sentence I'd ever heard. Wordy and precise. Cold."

He cleared his throat.

"I've been thinking about that answer lately. When you don't know answers that you should know, it really does come down to clarity. Achieving clarity. It's actually a precise description of the process of understanding."

Remmick looked down as he swallowed and breathed in deeply.

"Achieving clarity. The second to last step in achieving truth."

Remmick looked relaxed and confident now. He was looking the day of reckoning in the eye.

Arnie had a puzzled look, eyes darting around at various individuals, searching for some recognition from someone. He didn't know what Remmick was talking about. Father Tim's look would best be described as hopeful, eyes lit, brow raised as though waiting to hear a punchline.

Remmick gazed once more at Maggie. She was sitting with her back straight, hands on her lap, eyes locked on him. Her face was bright, poised to smile, framed by her coiffed hair. Her chest heaved as her respiration rate became elevated. Remmick could read her mind. She was flush with anticipation as four years of sleeplessness and shittiness met on the ballfield right here. Maggie was desperate to feel something good.

"Contrary to what Mr. Ungar told you," Remmick began, then stopped, staring off beyond Maggie.

"I do not regret--"

The room was silent as a grave as Remmick continued in a subdued voice.

"--killing that fucking maggot--"

Eyes grew wider.

"--who abused, threatened and assaulted--"

Ungar's eyes peered up from under dark brows.

"--a perfectly good human being."

Maggie's mouth was open, her eyes ice cold.

"His exercise of power and control over Hilde Schimmel terrorized her. He blackmailed her for months. She couldn't fight him. And when she tried to leave, he tossed her into a glass table."

Maggie had closed her mouth but still looked shell-shocked. The Widow Morone sobbed quietly. Richard Morone looked satisfied.

"She gave herself to him, but he wanted more. She didn't know how to give more."

Toohey and his partners were frozen in their seats, staring right through Remmick.

"So she got out the only way left to her."

Remmick was reading off a teleprompter in his head. He knew this script all too well.

"Therefore--"

He breathed in to gather his finish.

"--I'm glad he's dead. Four years in jail has been a small price to pay for erasing Ronald Morone from the planet."

The Widow Morone's sobbing halted. The only sound in the room was the creak of someone's wooden chair. Then, from Remmick's direction, a startling shout--

"EVERYBODY GOT THAT?"

The words echoed for what seemed like an eternity. They shook the Widow Morone who began crying loudly now. No one else made a sound. The three-member committee began stirring and Chairman Toohey finally spoke."

"Well, Mr. Remmick, I see we've come full circle," he said with a smirk. "Does anyone have anything to add?"

No one spoke.

"We're adjourned," said Toohey.

###

Chapter 21

The day Remmick got out, they gave him a new sweat suit, boxers, white sox, a pair of no-name sneakers and $100 in twenties. Father Timmons brought the items to his cell that morning. The CO unlocked the door and in Timmons walked, placing them on Remmick's cot. He then sat down as Remmick stood to step out of the prison jumpsuit and put on his new clothes. Timmons watched with his hands folded as Remmick quietly stepped into the sweat pants.

"You know," Timmons began, "this is the point where I usually say, God speed, brother, and good luck."

Remmick futzed with the drawstring, glancing only quickly at Timmons. Timmons' face was neutral.

"But not today."

Remmick gave an indifferent shrug, then sat down to put on his new socks and shoes.

"Say it, or don't," said Remmick. "I don't really care."

"It's humbling," continued Timmons, "to be in the presence of someone who wields the power of life and death without pause, without looking in the rear view mirror."

Timmons paused and put his hand on Remmick's arm. "Without remorse."

The shoes made that new-rubber squeak as Remmick's feet hit the floor and he stood again, glaring down at Timmons. His breathing quickened as he loaded up for a comeback, then decided not to.

"Father Timmons," Remmick began in the same low, even voice he used during his hearing. "In deference to the time you spent with me over these four years, the compassion you've shown me and the patience you exhibited by sharing room air with me, I will say only this: If you're here representing the same God that let Ronald Morone walk the face of the earth to beat his wife and drive Hilde Schimmel to kill herself, then get out of my sight and take God with you."

Timmons eyes had been locked on Remmick's. As the last words left Remmick's mouth, Timmons broke his gaze and looked into the virtual horizon for a response.

Remmick pulled the sweatshirt over his head, adjusted it around his waist and then picked up the cash and folded it, placing it into a pocket of the sweat pants.

"Please tell the CO's I'm ready. On your way out."

Father Timmons left the cell for the last time.

###

Epilogue

The day I got out wasn't the festival of lights I expected it to be. There was a vague feeling of angst mixed with exhaustion. It dawned on me that I was walking out of a place where attention was paid to me and into the wider world which didn't give a shit. The prison counselor tried to prepare me for the eventuality that I would be rejected for jobs because I had a record, but it didn't really hit me until the day I walked free. Who would want to hire me for anything other than wiping down cars coming out of the Bubble Tunnel?

Maggie met me at the gate, you know, like that scene in Goodfellas where Ray Liotta walks out of prison in a shiny suit and Lorraine Bracco greets him? Only differences--my clothes were lame, Maggie's car was lame and she wasn't exactly posing like a debutante. I think, in fact, that she wasn't all that thrilled to be there. She aged in four years, thanks to me. There was a distant hint of the Maggie smile of old, a pretense for my benefit, of course.

I got a hug, a real one, then a real kiss. It was a delicious moment that warmed me to my core. I wouldn't let the hug end.

"Jeez, it's like you've been in jail or something," she quipped.

I pulled back a bit to look into her eyes. Those eyes hadn't changed, thank god.

"In four years, I never said it," I said softly. "Thank you."

She just looked back at me and nodded slightly, then turned towards her Subaru and got into the driver's seat. I walked to the passenger side and let myself in. We sat together in that car. The last time we had done that was during the trip to report to prison.

"The apartment's nice, though not huge," she said while staring straight ahead at the road. "It'll work."

"I'm sure," I said. "I can't wait." I turned to her and repeated, "I really can't."

"Oh man, you're not gonna launch into how it's gonna be a whole new start for us, are you? I mean, that speech isn't going to--"

"No," I interrupted. "No speeches. I'm just grateful."

Maggie reached for my hand as we settled in for the three-hour drive across I-80, deep into Pennsylvania.

###

CPSIA information can be obtained
at www.ICGtesting.com
Printed in the USA
BVOW08s0746150118
505268BV00001B/264/P